NUDES

A Hollywood Romance

Sarah Robinson

*To every woman who was called a slut
while her lover was congratulated.*

TABLE OF CONTENTS

PROLOGUE

Aria woke with a jolt, looking around the dark bedroom. As her senses slowly began to adjust, she looked for the source of whatever had disturbed her. Her cell phone vibrated against the surface of her nightstand, the screen lit so brightly it cast a square light onto the ceiling above.

Yawning, Aria grabbed for it. She glanced over at the man in bed next to her, her heart filling with warmth at the sight of his sleeping form.

Finally focusing on her phone, she realized she had dozens of missed texts, calls, and emails.

"What the hell?" she whispered to herself, sitting up.

Aria, are you awake? WAKE UP NOW.
Don't look at the news. We need to talk. 911.
Is that you on E! News? Did you allow that?
OMG, ARIA! WHAT THE HELL?
What did you do?!?! This is career suicide!

1

Her heart began to race, panic swarming her every cell as she quickly clicked out on a website link her best friend sent her. A photo popped up, and then another, and another, and another, and Aria knew exactly what she was looking at.

Herself.

Nude.

Aria could barely breathe, trembling as she searched social media and entertainment news sites. The photos were everywhere. She was everywhere. Her breasts, her body, her love life on full display for the world to see.

It would have been bad enough if they'd just been images of her posing, but these were pornographic. These were her in her most intimate moments with a man she'd...

A sob stuck in her throat. *Did he do this?*

She looked at the man still sleeping beside her, fear gripping her heart.

This couldn't be happening.

.

CHAPTER ONE
TWO MONTHS EARLIER

"Wait until you meet our lead." The heavyset producer's eyes glinted with excitement as he spoke. He brought a sandwich up to his lips, taking a bite and continuing around a mouthful of food. "She's only had small roles up until this film, but she's up-and-coming. No doubt about it. Aria Rose is poised to take the world by storm come Oscar season."

Ben didn't reply, too distracted watching the producer trying to wipe a blob of mayonnaise off his tie. Arthur Atwood was a large man with a messy comb-over and an ill-fitting suit, which must have been a deliberate choice since Ben knew Arthur made a handsome salary.

Is he licking his tie?

His new right-hand man was actually licking mayonnaise off his tie. Not a good sign. Ben made a mental note never to ask Arthur to have a meeting over lunch at his desk again.

"Bugger, it's in there good," Arthur muttered in his thick English accent, dropping his tie and slapping his hands on his knees. "All right. Enough of that. Ready for a tour of the studio?"

"Very," Ben replied, balling up the parchment paper his own sandwich had been wrapped in and tossing it into the wastebasket beneath his desk. He stood, rolling his shoulders and stretching his neck from side to side.

They'd spent the morning touring the corporate offices on the lot of Shepherd Film Studios where Ben would be officially starting in two weeks as the company's new chief executive officer. He had agreed to come in on Friday to tour everything and meet the crew on their final day of filming—but the pressure was already on.

One of the oldest movie production companies in Hollywood, Shepherd Film Studios was well respected, but struggled to adapt to new changes in the industry—the rise of streaming services, quicker distribution on the internet, and other changes that appealed to younger generations.

Maguire Industries had recently purchased the studio and placed Ben in charge to fix that. He had one year to prove to the board at Maguire that he could turn Shepherd Films back into a thriving production company or they'd dismantle the company and sell it off for profit.

He was Shepherd Films last resort, and thank goodness, too. No one else in Hollywood was desperate enough to throw him a lifeline. Being an embarrassing public spectacle for the last two years had been by far one of the biggest setbacks in his professional life to date—and his personal life was to blame.

Fucking divorce.

"Have you seen any of her movies?" Arthur held the door to the office open for him, and together they headed down the hallways of the main offices. "She's a bombshell—literally one of the most gorgeous women I've ever seen."

"Aria Rose?" Ben replied, racking his brain for a mental image of the actress. "I've seen a few. Very pretty. She's very talented but never been a lead."

"*Scarlet's Letters* is her first starring role, and she's perfect for it. We can watch the dailies from today's filming, and you'll see what I mean. We were really lucky to score her for this film."

Ben had wondered about that, too. Aria wasn't necessarily A-list, but she was an up-and-coming fan favorite among millennial and younger generations. Her social media attention was nonstop, and there was an almost cult following to her that had made Hollywood execs begin to take notice. Yet, he'd seen the budget this morning. She was being vastly underpaid for this film, and he wasn't sure why.

They passed the guards at the front desk of the main offices and stepped out into the sun. "How did your team manage to sign her?" Ben asked.

"Sheer luck, I'd gather. She was following the script around—or so I heard. Determined to be part of it, though I can't say why exactly. The script is great—historical World War II romance with a Hester Prynne theme—and we're already getting some Oscar buzz from it. Still, it's a long shot, and it's nothing like her previous films."

Ben pulled a pair of sunglasses from his suit pocket and placed them over his eyes. The bright Los Angeles sun was beating down on them as they climbed onto a golf cart to traverse the large lot to the studios. "Sounds like we're the lucky ones, then."

"You've got that right," Arthur agreed, taking the driver's seat since Ben was still mostly unfamiliar with the area.

A few minutes later, their golf cart pulled up outside a large warehouse-type building that read *STUDIO E* in large black letters across the top. Ben climbed out and followed Arthur to a small door off to the side, a red light lit above the door.

Arthur pointed to the light. "That means they're filming, so not a peep." He placed a finger to his mouth, indicating they needed to be quiet.

Ben nodded, and they entered the building only to be immediately shrouded in darkness. It might be his first day at Shepherd Films, but Ben was no stranger to movie sets and felt immediately at ease as they carefully made their way over to where the camera crew was.

Ben's father, Roger Lawson, was a highly sought after cameraman who'd taken a career most people overlooked and became the best. He'd taught Ben to do the same—excel in everything by putting his whole heart into every project, no matter how small or large. As a young boy, he'd spent many a summer day with his father at work, learning the business of not only filming, but creating movies, in general.

Newly thirty years old, Ben had spent the last decade putting his father's words into practice, rising through the ranks to become one of the hottest names in film production. He only wished his father was still alive to see his ascent, or at least, he had wished that until his ex-wife smeared his name through the tabloids during their divorce.

Never fall in love with an actress. The one rule his father had told him before he died that Ben had ignored. Lesson learned.

"Am I to be punished for helping a fellow human being?" A strong female voice broke through the silence around them.

Ben stepped around a crowd of onlookers to see the set. Behind him was an entire crew, and not a single dry eye. The emotion on everyone's face surprised him. Following their attention to the main set, he saw the set was a bedroom. Sitting on the edge of the bed was a tall, broad-shouldered man with his head in his hands, wearing a soldier's uniform from the 1940's.

In front of the downtrodden soldier was a statuesque blonde, her hair flowing down her back in one long, chunky braid. Pieces of her golden mane escaped the braid, framing her face and highlighting her soft, pink cheeks. Pale blue-gray eyes brimmed with tears as she folded her hands over her heart.

"I won't lie, James," she continued, her voice softer now. "I can't."

The soldier suddenly stood, gripping the woman by her upper arms. "You have to lie, Anna. Your life is at stake—my life, *our life*. You'll be imprisoned, and everything we've dreamt of will be over."

She steeled herself, her jaw tightening. "If this is real...if our love is real...then we'll survive this. Without the lies, the tricks, the falsehoods. We can survive this, James."

Ben felt a swelling in his chest, a lump in his throat. He wasn't even sure what the storyline was about, and yet, he was captivated by the woman in front of the cameras. Her presence was powerful...*she* was powerful.

"No, Anna." He dropped her arms and stepped back, a look of disgust on his face. "We can't survive this. Not if you choose their lives over mine...over ours."

The blonde shook her head slowly, her hand now on her stomach as if she might be sick. "You can't mean that, James. You can't make me pick between loving you and my purpose in life."

"It's them...or it's me. Now or never, Anna."

Ben focused on the actress's face, expecting to see her acquiesce to the steely-delivered ultimatum. Instead, her chin pushed up and she inhaled deeply. Everything about her posture and stance screamed strength, and yet, in the exact same moment, those blue-gray eyes ached with pain. Ben nearly forgot he was watching actors because her portrayal was so genuine...she was so genuine.

"Goodbye, James." Her voice was gentle, but resolute.

The soldier's nostrils flared angrily, before he slowly shook his head. "Goodbye, Anna." With that, he walked out of the door and left her standing alone in the bedroom.

She waited a moment, staring after him. Her hand slowly lifted to her lips, covering her mouth as a loud sob ripped from her throat. In an excruciating display, her body dipped forward slightly before completely crumpling in on itself. She fell against the edge of the bed, sobbing into its sheets, as the lights on set dimmed.

"Cut!" the director yelled. "Holy fuck. That was amazing, Aria!"

The blond actress pushed up off the bed, smiling and wiping the tears from her cheeks. Everyone in the studio erupted into applause, and Ben joined in. She deserved every second of it after that performance.

A surge of excitement ran through Ben's body—he could do this. With acting like this, there was no way their movie wouldn't be a success. There was no way he wouldn't be able to bring this studio success within the year with a film like this.

"Hey, Russell," Arthur called out to the director and ushered Ben over to him. "Meet our new studio head, Ben Lawson."

Ben extended a hand to the grungy looking man with long, curly black hair to his shoulders. "Good to meet you, Russell."

"Please, call me Russ. I'm Russ Rains, director. I'm sure you've heard of me." He donned a cocky smile. Metal and bracelets around his wrists made a clanking sound as they shook hands—a not too unusual fashion choice in this city.

"I have," Ben admitted, though he didn't really like this man's ego already. It was certainly nothing unusual in Hollywood, and Ben had met the type many a time before. Russell Rains was a legitimately well-known director with several big box office hits under his belt, though it had been many years since his last. "Your work is amazing, Russ."

"Thank you, Benji," Russ said with an obnoxious chuckle. "Come on. Let me introduce you to our leads."

"I'll meet you back at the office," Arthur told Ben. "Have fun on set!"

Ben followed Russell onto the bedroom set where the actress he'd been so captivated by was hugging the soldier who'd just broken her heart.

"You were amazing, Travis," she said to him, pulling back from their embrace to smile at him.

Something inside Ben stirred — irritation, anger? He wasn't sure, but he didn't like seeing the man's arms around the beautiful blonde.

"Sweet pea, come meet our new studio head," Russ called out to Aria, who visibly bristled at his demand. Ben made a mental note to ask about the director's dynamic with the actors later. "This here is Benji."

"*Ben* Lawson," Ben corrected the director, extending his hand to the woman.

"Aria Rose," she replied, taking his hand with a gentle squeeze. Her fingers were small and warm around his, and there was something sad about letting go. "Pleased to meet you, Mr. Lawson. This is my co-star, Travis Peters."

The soldier shook his hand next. "Good to meet you, sir."

"Please, call me Ben," he instructed them both. "Travis, you were fantastic. And, Aria, I have to admit that your performance just now was incredible. I was unbelievably moved."

Her pale pink cheeks darkened as she looked down at her hands. "Thank you."

"I have no doubt this movie will be phenomenal."

Russ slapped a hand on Ben's back. "Hell, yeah. That was our last scene, so we're officially wrapped." The director stepped away from them and yelled to the entire crew. "It's a wrap, fuckers!"

Ben didn't even cringe at the man's abrasiveness this time.

The crew clapped and cheered, and everyone was hugging and high-fiving each other. A swarm of people came onto the bedroom set to congratulate Aria, pushing Ben backward as he watched her gracefully accept their praise.

In fact, he couldn't take his eyes off her, and it only had a little to do with how unbelievably attracted he was to her. As he stepped to the side, he watched how she smiled, laughing and embracing her co-workers. It was captivating. Aria commanded a room, not just when she was acting, but as herself. Her eyes danced and shone as she spoke to the crew and other actors, her smile wide and transformative.

He felt drawn to who she was, not just what he saw, and it was intoxicating. Though, what he saw was certainly breathtaking. Gorgeous wasn't enough to describe this woman, or the way her long neck dipped into thin shoulders and a deep collarbone. Her breasts pushed against the dark red dress she was wearing that highlighted her hourglass silhouette, and her golden braid hung down over her shoulder with a weight and visible softness he'd never seen before.

Someone bumped Ben's shoulder as they rushed in her direction, bringing Ben back to reality. *What the fuck am I doing?* He was barely six months out of a long divorce and had sworn off women entirely for now. And an actress? That was not happening. No way would he repeat his previous mistake twice. Not to mention that he was her boss, essentially, and that it would be a major conflict of interest. That was even assuming she was single and interested in him, which...

Why am I even thinking about this? Ben shook the thought from his head, unsure when the last time was that he'd ever felt this foggy-headed over a woman.

Aria's laughter peeled through the air just then, melodic and joyous. Ben swallowed hard, shoving his hands in his pockets and heading for the door. He had to get out of there. Now.

He wouldn't let himself fall for another actress, not even one as beautiful as Aria Rose.

CHAPTER TWO

"Congratulations, sweetie!" Betty Reynolds, Aria's mother, rushed over to her and threw her arms around her neck. "You were *amazing*. There was no doubt, of course, but my God, sweetheart! You're a star!"

"Ma! Too tight!" Aria gasped, but hugged her mother back.

Her mother held her at arm's length. "Look at you." She exhaled loudly, smiling dreamily at her. "Seriously, Aria. You are so talented."

Aria felt her cheeks heat and looked away, never one to be very comfortable with praise. "Ma..."

"I'm serious, baby girl. The most talented actress I've ever seen."

Aria laughed, but welcomed her mother's input anyway. At times, Betty Reynolds may be overly involved in her life, but she'd prefer that than to not have her at all. In fact, Betty was not only her mother but her manager. She'd hired her years ago and hadn't regretted it for a second, probably because no one would ever work as hard or fight as fiercely for her. Aria credited a lot of her own success to her mother for that. "Thank you, Ma. I'm happy we're wrapped, though."

"Well, given your history on set..." Betty glanced toward the director, Russell Rains, who was currently talking to one of the cameramen. "It's understandable that you'd want to be out of here."

Aria pulled her gaze from Russ, her stomach turning at the thought. No one else in her family but her mother knew that she'd dated Russell for the first three months of filming. He was brilliant and intense, and she'd gotten swept up in the passion of it all, mixing her real emotions into the scripted life he led. She'd been so naive—a harsh fact she'd learned when she'd found him with an intern's head bobbing up and down in his lap.

Since breaking things off with Russell, she'd found him unbelievably difficult to work with. He'd made it very clear he resented the fact that she'd initiated their end—as if she was the first woman to ever reject him. It had made for an uncomfortable last few months of filming, but she'd done her best to ignore his passive aggressive barbs and blatant advances.

All things considered, she was really happy with her own performance, even if she hadn't seen the final product yet.

"This movie is going to be big, Aria. I can *feel* it."

Aria wrapped an arm around her mother's shoulders as they walked in the direction of the dressing rooms. "From your lips to God's ears."

When they arrived at her room, a small room with no windows on the second floor of a long row of dressing rooms, Aria dropped down on the couch with a big sigh. "I could sleep forever."

"Why don't you take a nap before heading home?" Betty asked, her eyes on her watch. "I've got to get home to relieve your father's nurse for the evening."

"Oh, go, go. Don't let me keep you." Aria pulled her feet onto the couch and pushed a pillow under her head, curling up for a nap. "I probably will rest my eyes for a minute."

Betty grabbed a throw blanket off a nearby chair and draped it over her. "Okay, sweetheart. I love you."

"Love you, Ma," Aria said, already drifting off to sleep. They'd been filming since four in the morning today, trying to finish the last scene. Now that it was over, she felt like she could sleep for days.

Darkness fell over the room, and Aria felt her body relax, slipping out of consciousness. Minutes, hours, she wasn't sure how long she'd slept before she was jolted awake.

"Oh, shit. Were you sleeping?"

Sitting up, Aria blinked and rubbed her eyes. Russell was standing in the doorway of her dressing room, a wicked grin on his face.

"What do you want, Russ?" She kept her tone flat, her teeth clenched.

"You coming to the wrap party tonight?"

Aria yawned, checking the clock on the wall. She'd apparently been sleeping for three hours — much longer than a nap. "Yeah, I'm going."

She was feeling refreshed after the extra hours of rest, and she did want to celebrate with the crew — even if that meant enduring another few hours of her ex-boyfriend.

Russ glanced up and down the hallway outside the room, then stepped in and closed the door behind him. "Hey, maybe we should have a celebration of our own..."

Aria immediately got to her feet. "Get. Out."

"Come on, baby," he cooed, crossing the room. "Don't you miss us? The film's wrapped, and we can get back to being us outside of work."

"*Us* was over the moment I caught you fooling around with an intern," she seethed, instantly angry that he still couldn't take a hint.

Russ's face glowered, going from sexual to angry. "Whatever. I've got a good memory." He winked at her and gestured first to his head, and then to his crotch as if he was jerking off.

Aria's stomach turned. "You're disgusting."

He shrugged while he walked back to the door, nonchalantly. Looking back over his shoulder, his face split into a wicked smile. "You'll be back. D-List actresses always come back for this dick when they realize I'm the best they'll ever have."

"Fuck you," Aria shot out, crossing her arms over her chest.

With his signature sinister smile, he walked out of the dressing room.

Aria's insides boiled. *Slime*. He was complete and utter slime. Clearly, she'd lost her damn mind when she'd briefly dated him. She'd been so easily mesmerized by his talent as a director, and he'd taught her so much. She'd thought it was just innocent, but all those extra late night lessons had turned into him hitting on her and her...just going with it.

Groaning, Aria dropped back onto the couch. *God, I'm so stupid.* She couldn't believe she'd been fooled by someone as blatantly slimy as him.

"Hey, Aria!" A silver-haired beauty bounced into the room through the doorway Russ had just exited.

"Hi, Steele," Aria greeted her makeup artist and hair stylist, who was really more like her best friend after spending every day together over the past few months of filming. Steele was her full name—or so she insisted—*like Cher*, she always said.

Steele collapsed onto the couch next to her, leaving a puff of glitter in the air. "Today is the absolute worst."

"What? Why?" Aria turned to her friend, pulling her legs up on the couch to face her.

Steele was uniquely gorgeous, the kind of beauty that was all personality, too. Brightly dyed silver hair, colorful makeup, ears lined with half a dozen earrings each, and vibrantly colored clothes made her stand out in any room. Her always exuberant attitude matched her style, and the two had quickly grown close.

"It's our last day," Steele said, her voice exaggeratedly whining. "Friendship over!"

Aria laughed, tipping her head back at her friend's dramatics. "Our friendship is not over! It's the last day of filming, but you know I'm going to need you again. There's still the photo shoot for promos for the film. There's the red carpet look. Press events. There's a ton of things I still need you for."

"Oh, great," Steele teased, tossing her hands up. "So, we're only friends because you still need me."

"Aside from being the best makeup artist and hair stylist in town, I have no use for you," Aria said in mock seriousness. "Honestly, you're just in the way otherwise."

Steele squawked. "Bitch."

"You know I'm kidding!" Aria leaned her head on Steele's shoulder, hugging her arm. "I love you, girl. We're still friends even if we aren't working together."

"Ugh." Steele squirmed away and stood up. "That's enough mushy gushy for now. I don't do *feelings*."

Aria grinned, fully aware that Steele was a lot more emotional than she let on. "Whatever, crazy. Help me pick out an outfit and look for the wrap party tonight."

"Now *that* I can do." Steele was already pulling clothes apart on the rack to one side of the room. "Let's go slutty tonight."

"I'm not going slutty," Aria countered, thinking of Russ's attendance.

Steele sighed. "You always turn down slutty. What about half slutty?"

"What's half slutty?"

Steele held up a dress that had no cleavage. It completely covered her chest and wrapped her neck, leaving only her arms and shoulders bare.

Aria frowned. "How is that half slutty?"

Steele held it up against her body and indicated the hem at the bottom. It barely touched the top of her thighs.

Laughing, Aria shook her head. "So, I'm a nun on top and then naked on the bottom?"

"Exactly. Half slutty."

Aria took the dress and held it up to her own body. It went a little lower on her because she was shorter than Steele, reaching about mid-thigh. "Pair these with knee-high boots to cover my legs and I'll wear it."

Steele pumped her fist through the air. "Finally! Maybe you'll meet a guy tonight."

"I am *not* dating right now," Aria countered, closing the dressing room door so she could get changed. "Not even interested."

"Imagine how pissed Russ would be if he saw you with another guy though." Steele handed her a set of suede boots that matched the emerald green cocktail dress perfectly. "It's the perfect revenge for his cheating ass."

Not many people knew about her affair with Russ, but Steele was part of her inner circle. Still, she had no desire to make Russell jealous. She just wanted him gone.

"I think I've learned my lesson about dating people I work with," Aria countered, lifting her shirt over her head and tossing it onto the couch. "And there's no one here I'd want to date anyway."

Steele shrugged. She was lining makeup on the counter. "There was a new guy on set today. Sexy as hell in that suit. I might have to call dibs on that."

"You're engaged," Aria reminded her. She had to admit though, Steele was right. Shepherd Film's new CEO was handsome as hell. So handsome, in fact, that she'd already completely blanked on his name from when he introduced himself. His smoldering blue eyes, rugged jaw, and broad shoulders had completely eclipsed her attention for a moment.

Steele winked at her in her reflection in the mirror as she stood behind Aria and zipped up the back of the dress. "Engaged, not blind. Sit. I'm going to do a smoky eye tonight."

"Like you'd ever leave Xavier. I've never seen two people more in love." Aria grabbed Steele's phone off the counter, clicking it on to show her the background photo. It was of Steele and a tattooed man kissing, arms wrapped around each other.

Steele blushed and took her phone back. "It's true. We're really fucking cute." Aria sat still as Steele began wiping off the makeup from filming. "And I'm about to make you really fucking cute, so you better not waste it on another night alone with your battery-operated boyfriend."

She giggled, feeling her face flush with heat. "Steele!"

Part of her had to admit, she wasn't as closed off to dating and men as she let on. She was focused on her career and not about to let a man get in the way of that, but it would be really nice to have someone to fall asleep next to again.

The truth was, Aria was lonely, and she was starting to think it was time to do something about that.

CHAPTER THREE

"Thank you," Aria said to the cocktail waiter who handed her a glass of champagne the moment she walked onto the yacht. The studio had rented out an insanely large yacht docked in the Marina del Ray in Los Angeles for the entire crew to celebrate the wrap of production, and Aria was already overwhelmed by the size of the crowd onboard.

It wasn't that she wasn't a social person, but rather, a bit of an introvert. She'd been up since four in the morning working on a busy set with hundreds of people, so her energy level was pretty drained already.

"Aria!" Travis, her co-star and close friend, waved to her from the front of the ship. "Come join us!"

She made her way toward him, squeezing past groups of people and downing half her champagne. "Hey, guys."

"You remember our new CEO, Ben Lawson, right?" Travis pointed to a man whose back was to her. "Ben, you know Aria Rose."

When he turned, she was confronted by the same smoldering blue eyes she'd been mesmerized by earlier in the day. But, he was different. Calmer. Relaxed, even. He wore dark jeans and a collared shirt that wasn't buttoned completely to the top, and his chin was scruffy, as if he'd shaved that morning but it had already begun to grow back. As attracted as she had been to the suited stranger before, she was even more enthralled by the rugged man standing before her now.

"Of course," Ben replied, extending a hand in her direction. "Wonderful to see you again, Ms. Rose."

Aria took his hand, letting it linger in his large grasp a moment longer than necessary. "It's actually Reynolds. Rose is my stage name."

"Interesting," Ben replied, his eyes raking over her body not so subtly. She felt her skin warming, suddenly feeling fidgety. "Is Aria your real name, too?"

"It is," she replied, unsure why she was even telling him this. Most people weren't privy to her personal life at all, and yet she felt an immediate desire to have him know her. "I use a stage name to stand apart from my cousin. He's a famous actor, and I wanted to make my own way in this industry."

"Didn't want to ride his coattails...very admirable."

"Thank you." She tipped the remainder of the glass of champagne past her lips, finishing the glass. Before she could even clear her throat, Travis was already handing her another.

"No drink limit tonight!" Travis wiggled his brows. "Mr. Hot Shot CEO here hired sober rides for anyone who needs it."

Aria glanced at Ben, his gaze cast down with a small smile on his lips. He wasn't embarrassed by Travis's admiration, but he clearly wasn't looking for praise either. She liked that level of confidence in a man, or in any person.

"Sober rides, huh?" Russell Rains suddenly appeared in the circle and tossed an arm around Ben's shoulders. "Trying to win them over before your first day, Benji? It's working!"

Travis laughed. "He's got my vote—and my car keys."

Stepping back slightly, Aria tried to blend into the crowd behind her. The moment the group's focus no longer included her, she pivoted and put as much distance between herself and Russ as she could.

Hard to do on a yacht.

Finding solace at the bow of the ship, Aria was now in a much smaller crowd. Lights were dimmer, music was softer, and the few people there were having intimate conversation rather than the raucous party happening at the back of the boat.

Aria inhaled the ocean air and leaned against the railing, her elbows propped against it. Water crashed against the side of the yacht in a lazy, rhythmic manner that entranced her for a moment. It was serene and beautiful, and her mind began to drift to everything the last few months had brought her.

She'd done a few small movies before this one, never big budget and never a starring role. Growing up in Los Angeles, the daughter of a low-budget cinema owner, watching movies hadn't just been a hobby—it was her whole childhood. Her father often let her and her sisters tag along to work with him, leaving them to sneak in and out of theaters all day. She fell in love with the silver screen young, and that passion never left her.

"Aria?" A deep voice cut through the crisp nighttime air.

She turned to see Ben approaching her, the shadows from the upper deck of the yacht moving across his face as he came closer. "Oh. Hi, Mr. Lawson."

"Please, like I said, call me Ben," he reiterated, leaning against the railing next to her.

"Right. Ben. Sorry, the last exec wasn't quite so..."

His lips curved into a smile. "So, what?"

She wasn't sure what to say, because her honest answer was *sexy*. That didn't seem like the best thing to a man who now funded and controlled her film. "Approachable?"

Ben laughed—a deep chuckle that she felt vibrate through her bones. "I hope that's a good thing."

"It definitely is," she assured him, placing a hand on his arm. The moment she touched him, she pulled back, immediately embarrassed.

He. Is. My. Boss. Get it together, Aria.

He didn't chide her, or look uncomfortable, which she took as a good sign.

Aria returned to her original position beside him, and they stared out at the darkened water lapping the sides of all the boats docked around.

"Want to hear something funny?" Aria finally broke the silence, but kept her voice low. So low, he had to lean in to hear her.

"Tell me."

"My parents met in this very marina. She was a caterer and he was a deckhand—still teenagers. Barely old enough to know who they were, let alone what they wanted out of life. Still, they knew what love was when they stumbled upon it, and they knew enough to never let go." Aria's heart beat a little faster, warming at the memories.

"Wow. Are they still together?"

Aria nodded. "Barely spent a day apart since. My mother is actually my manager, and she works insanely hard for me, but my father always comes first. He's the love of her life."

"Love like that is special. Rare."

"Is it?" Aria tilted her head to the side. "I'm not sure it's as rare as it is a choice, a commitment, and the strength to follow through each and every day. There were times they could have given up— maybe lived an easier life with someone else—but they made a decision that this was the love they wanted, this was the life they wanted, and in that choice comes a confidence, a happiness, that most people deny themselves."

Ben was quiet for a minute. Finally, he inhaled loudly, then blew it out in one long breath. "That's really beautiful, Aria. Hits a bit close to home, I have to admit."

"I'm sorry." Aria frowned, turning to face him and just leaving one elbow on the railing. "I didn't mean—"

He shook his head. "No, it's fine. I just finished going through a divorce about six months ago, though we'd separated the year before that. I think you're right—love is a choice. Making love work is a choice. And yet...if it's not with the right person, then it's the wrong choice."

"Soul mates." Aria raised one brow. "You believe in that?"

Ben stared at her for a moment...a long moment. The kind of moment that made her shift her weight from one leg to the other, her skin heating under his gaze. "Yes. I believe in soul mates."

She tilted her chin up ever so slightly, going for lightheartedness. "Well, we all have our flaws. You couldn't be entirely perfect."

Ben laughed again. "Believing in soul mates is a flaw?"

"Buying what you're selling is definitely a flaw. You're a movie producer, so you sell fantasy to the world."

"I think we can have the fantasy." His eyes danced, but his smile was gone. "Don't you want the fantasy?"

Aria turned back to the ocean, looking out at the waves. This was too much, too real, too soon with a man she barely knew. A man who was pretty much her boss. "Who wouldn't want the fantasy?" she said dismissively. "Some would say I'm already living it."

"That's certainly true. Everyone on this yacht, everyone in this city...Hollywood. It's all a fantasy of some sort." Something in his tone sounded so...sad? A small ache pulled at her heart, and she felt like they'd opened the door to something different. Something different than studio exec and actress. Something more than strangers who just met today.

Her humanity connected to his, and they were just two people standing on a boat wishing it could float them away from their picture-perfect lives.

"Do you know why I love *Scarlet's Letters*?" she said softly, her voice barely above the whistle of the wind around them.

He stepped closer, his elbow pressed against hers on the railing now. "Why?"

"It's something I can be proud of. A story I'm proud to tell. The strength of a woman in wartime, a French woman saving innocent people during the Holocaust...a woman picking her truth over a man, over love. Have you read the script?"

Ben nodded. "I have. Two years ago, when it was making the rounds. It's powerful, and from what I've seen, you do an amazing job in it."

"Thank you. When I first saw this script—or rather, read the book it's based on—I knew I had to play this part. No matter what I had to give up. This was mine."

She'd never connected to anything more than she had this script. It was empowering, and taught courage in the toughest of circumstances. It was a tiny snapshot of a much larger scale event, showing the decisions and atrocities suffered at such a human, personal level. It was a woman denying her own privilege and luxury to help fellow humans who didn't have that reach.

"The way you talk about it...I'm jealous," Ben admitted.

That got Aria's attention, and she turned to face him. "Jealous? Of what?"

He pushed off the railing, looking up at the stars before settling on her gaze. "Passion. Excitement. Purpose. You know what you want. You know who you are and what your goals are."

"And you don't?" He had to be nearly thirty, if not over. Striking and fresh faced, but his features still said experience. Aria was only in her twenties, but at times she felt decades older.

Ben shook his head. "I thought I did. I built a life. Got married. Worked my way up in Maguire Industries. Everything was mapped out. Everything was...easy."

The ache from earlier was back, the sadness in his voice. Aria placed her hand on his forearm, a comforting gesture. Partly for him, but mostly for her. She needed a physical connection when they were connecting on so much more.

"What happened?" she pried, squeezing his arm ever so slightly.

Ben looked down at her hand, his eyes lingering. He didn't move or pull away, and when he lifted his head to face her again, there was a need in his eyes that made her insides heat. "The woman I trusted with all my secrets? She sold them to the highest bidder the moment I wasn't able to be a stepping stone for her career."

Aria didn't reply, sensing there was more.

"She used every connection she had to get me blacklisted. Took everything. Now Maguire Industries acquired Shepherd Films, expecting me to fail. Pushing me out."

"Not many would call being the CEO of a film studio a demotion," Aria pointed out.

"When you're used to being the landscaper, it's hard to become the rose."

Aria laughed, letting go of his arm. "First, soul mates. Now, roses. You're a poetic man, Ben Lawson. A true romantic."

Suddenly, his fingers intertwined with hers, pulling her to him. Pressing her body to his, chest to chest, heartbeat to heartbeat. His eyes never left hers, and she watched him wrestle with something...doubt, uncertainty. As if he didn't know why he'd just hugged her to him, but then need. Pure need darkened his eyes as something deeper pushed the rest away.

Her breath was lost as she concentrated on standing, her knees already threatening to buckle. She'd taken every second of the journey with him, and now she wanted more. Something about the way he smelled ignited every nerve ending in her body. The way he held her, one arm wrapped around her back, was so secure, so comfortable, so protective, so intimately. No one had ever held her like *that* in her entire life.

She didn't want him to let go.

He was fire. She wanted to leap into his flames.

"And what are you, Aria Rose?" Ben's fingers tipped her chin upward, her eyes finding his. "Who are you?"

The words rumbled in his chest, vibrating against him as he spoke. There was a genuineness to it that terrified her, unnerved her, and completely overwhelmed her. Their souls were laid bare and he was asking for more.

A perfect stranger. A moment of truth. An absolute mistake.

She couldn't do it. Her walls shot up and she let go of him, fear coursing through her. "I'm an actress, Mr. Lawson. Just an actress."

And just so much more.

CHAPTER FOUR

Ben was still two days away from officially starting his new job at Shepherd Film Studios, and he had already almost fucked it up his first day on the lot.

Lesson learned, my ass.

Two weeks ago at the wrap party, he'd come insanely close to kissing Aria Rose. *Aria-fucking-Rose.* He'd spent every day since then preparing for his new job, ingratiating himself to the board of Maguire Industries, and doing everything he could to erase that gorgeous woman from his mind.

The number of ways that would be inappropriate were never ending. She was, essentially, his employee. She was also the face of his company's biggest project at the moment. His future in the film industry, and the entire future of Shepherd's Film Studios, rested on the success — or failure — of *Scarlet's Letters*.

The moment he'd realized how close he was to pressing his lips to hers, he'd let go and taken off. Literally. Just turned and walked away without saying a thing. *Fucking asshole.* She must have been so confused. Or irritated. Or plain mad. He had no idea, and certainly hadn't stayed around to find out.

Now he was spending his second Saturday since in his future office, prepping for Monday. Reading scripts, looking over marketing plans, budgets, staff, prepping what he'd say in the staff meeting on his first day—there was no end to the amount of work that would be on his plate.

In truth, he didn't mind a heavy workload. Staying busy kept his mind from wandering, his heart from aching. It was too quiet at home, and too empty inside. Hell, it was too quiet in this office.

Pushing away from his desk, Ben stood and stretched his arms over his head. No better time than now to explore the studios. Filming was wrapped and everyone was off for the weekend to celebrate, so he'd have the place to himself.

A couple minutes later, he was strolling across the sunny lot, taking it all in as he paced his way across the entire compound. Parking lots. Warehouses. Giant hangars with built sets inside. Outdoor sets. Offices. While certainly not the largest studio lot he'd been on, it was impressive. One of the oldest in Hollywood, but you wouldn't know it by the spectacular upkeep.

Ben came to the building where he'd watched Aria perform in her final scene. He tested the handle, finding it unlocked. *Probably should change that policy.*

Stepping inside, he was plunged into darkness. One single light came from the bend at the end of the hallway, and he made his way toward it.

"Damn it! Get off!"

Ben frowned, walking faster toward the muffled grunts and sounds coming from the end of the hallway.

"Did they glue it on here? What the hell?" the voice said again, louder and angrier this time.

Finally, Ben stepped around the corner and found Aria standing on the counter of a large kitchen set. She was holding a screwdriver, pushing it behind a plaque on the wall that looked like it was permanently attached.

"Do not make me come back here with a hammer," she threatened, still unaware of his presence.

Ben stifled a laugh, not wanting to alert her. *Was she talking to the wall? Wait...was she stealing that plaque from the set?* Ben couldn't stop the smile that spread over his face. This was too good.

"Would it help if I said please? Please, please let me rip you off the wall and steal you?"

Ben couldn't hold it one more moment, deciding to blow his cover. "SECURITY! STOP!"

"Ack!" Aria screamed and leapt backward, her feet missing the edge of the counter and causing her to tumble to the ground.

"Shit!" Ben rushed forward, reaching for her and grabbing her inches before she hit the ground. "Are you okay?"

She blinked a few times, looking up at him. "Ben? What the hell! You scared the crap out of me."

"Admittedly, not my most thought out prank."

Aria snorted, rolling her eyes. Pushing back up on to her feet, she shooed him away and he instantly missed the touch of her. Holding her that first night, and now...he could do that forever and not get bored.

"Well, great. The brand new big-man-on-campus catches me stealing. Fantastic."

Her sarcasm was so thick that he had to laugh. "I don't officially start until Monday, actually."

One perfectly arched brow raised. "Really? So, if I were to take this right now..."

"I couldn't do a thing about it," Ben replied with a shrug. Truthfully, she could take whatever she wanted and he'd let her have it.

"Perfect, then can you get it off for me? I swear, it's glued to the freaking wall." She pointed to a wooden plaque over the sink with a quote painted in white.

"Whatever our souls are made of, his and mine are the same." — Emily Brontë

Ben felt the corners of his lips twitch. "That plaque?"

Aria nodded. "Yep."

"The one about soul mates?" he clarified, a thrill running through his body at what felt like a victory. This couldn't be a coincidence. It couldn't.

She felt it, too.

"It's just a sweet phrase. Let's not read too much into it," Aria hastened her reply, her cheeks already turning bright red. Even the slightest of blushes stood out against her pale skin and blond hair. "I just wanted a memento from my time here."

Ben pulled a chair over to stand on and took the screwdriver from her, managing to get the plaque off the wall with a bit of finagling. Climbing back down, he handed it to her. "Whatever you say, Aria Rose."

She eyed him, clearly annoyed. "Do you have a few free minutes?"

"I can make time," he replied, though he technically had the whole day free.

"Good. Come with me." She motioned for him to follow her, then tucked the plaque against her chest and headed down a long corridor with doors on either side that had actors' names on them.

A few minutes later, they arrived at a door that read ARIA ROSE in big bold letters. She swung it open and stepped inside...into complete chaos. Clothes and boxes were strewn across every surface of the dimly lit room with no windows.

This is the dressing room they gave her? Ben made a mental note to change the crappy set up for upcoming films.

"Sorry about the mess. I'm packing my dressing room and taking it all home today." Aria waved around her at the piles of clothes. "Annnnd...I could use some help."

Crossing his arms over his chest, Ben leaned against the doorframe. "Are you asking the CEO of one of Hollywood's oldest and most prestigious studios to help you pack?"

"You're not the CEO yet." Aria's smile was teasing, wicked. He hadn't seen this side of her yet, but it might be his favorite. "In fact, you don't even work here right now. I'm pretty sure that means you're trespassing. Help me pack, and maaaaybe I won't call security."

He chuckled. "You make it hard to say no, don't you?"

"Do you really want to say no?" She picked up a box and tossed a pair of shoes into it.

"Not even a little." His answer came without a second thought.

She glanced at him, pausing at his words, or maybe his tone. The huskiness in his voice. Her lips twitched, but she hid her smile. "Well, grab a box then."

He did, and they spent the next thirty minutes in near silence, stuffing clothes in boxes and carrying them down to her car. There wasn't as much as he'd first thought, now that it was neatly packed into several boxes.

"That's the last of it." She closed the trunk of her car. "I'm officially all moved out."

"Are you going to miss it?" Ben turned to look at the building.

She took a deep breath then shook her head. "No. I won't. I'll be back."

The studio had a few other small budget movies currently filming, but nothing she was involved in. The next one set to film didn't have her on the cast list either. Though, he would certainly love any excuse to keep her around. "You will?"

"I will."

He wanted to push at her, tease her confidence. "What makes you so certain? This movie could tank and we'd never use you in another film again."

She didn't take the bait, turning dreamy, blue-gray eyes to his. "I'll be back."

Suddenly, every time he'd tried to push her out of his mind over the last two weeks broke down. She was too beautiful, too enticing, too mesmerizing.

He needed to feel her again. He needed to kiss her. He needed *her*.

Closing the gap between them, he stepped toward her. One hand on her back, pulling her against him; the other, cupping the side of her face. For a split second, they stared at each other, then, unable to resist, he pressed his lips to hers.

Soft. Slow. He waited for her response, for her to encourage him, to want him. She moaned, barely above a murmur, and leaned into his chest. It was all he needed to do what he'd wanted to do since the moment he'd first seen her on set.

He kissed her deeply, eagerly. She parted her mouth, and his tongue plunged inside, tasting everything she gave him.

Her hands twisted in his shirt—tighter, pulling, needing. She moaned against his lips, his tongue, his body.

Every doubt in his mind, every reason why they shouldn't be doing this...disappeared. Nothing about this felt wrong. She felt perfect. She felt like she'd been meant to be his all his life, and he was just realizing it now.

It was dizzying. Maddening.

When he pulled away, they were both panting and trying to regain their breath. Her chest rising and falling against him at a fast pace, distractingly provocative.

"Ben..." she breathed, blinking rapidly.

"I'm sorry." He tried to find a way to explain his complete break with sanity. "And I'm also not sorry at all. I've wanted to do that since the moment I saw you. And it's completely against the rules—if there even are rules. It's entirely unprofessional, and I should know better."

"You *should* know better," she agreed, her head tilted to the side and a small smile on her face. "But so should I."

He grinned, but kept his tone serious. "This shouldn't happen."

"It definitely shouldn't." She pulled her lips between her teeth and let go. Full pink lips that he'd just been kissing...and wanted to be kissing again. "It would be completely inappropriate."

Ben felt sure his entire body was about to explode. His jeans suddenly felt entirely too tight, and his skin entirely too hot.

Aria slid her tongue across her lower lip. "Or...maybe it's not?"

"I'm listening." *Anything*.

"Aside from some promotional photo shoots, yesterday was my last day here. And you..." Aria pointed squarely at him, the corners of her lips twitching. "You don't officially work here until Monday."

"We're free agents."

She nodded. "Only for two days."

Ben placed a hand on the trunk of her car. "You know, if you needed help loading all this in the car, then you'll probably need help unloading it at your house."

"You make a valid point, Mr. Lawson."

Ben's pulse quickened, his heart pounding in his chest.

Fuck. I'm in so much trouble.

CHAPTER FIVE

"That's the last one." Ben carefully placed the box he was carrying on the tile floor of Aria's foyer. Straightening, he scoped out her modest apartment. The location was ideal — overlooking Santa Monica Pier from the top floor of a slightly disheveled apartment complex. The interior, however, left a lot to be desired with outdated appliances, peeling wallpaper, and cramped quarters.

"Thanks." Aria closed the door behind her with her foot, her arms full with bags that she placed on top of the box. "Sorry about the place. It's small and crappy, I know."

Ben shook his head. "Honestly, I love it."

"Really?" Aria eyed him suspiciously. "Those jeans you're wearing probably cost as much as my rent."

Ben rubbed the back of his neck, feeling a bit self-conscious. "Because of the label, not the quality." He gestured around her home, stepping further into the living room. "It's small, sure, but it's homey. It's comfortable. This isn't just where you live...it's where you're home."

His own home was stoic and cold. Designer labels, expensive price tags, and absolutely nothing soft per his ex-wife's instructions when she decorated their house. Nothing felt lived in, or comforting, or...home.

Ben dropped onto the couch with a contented sigh, enjoying the feeling of sinking into the old cushions. It reminded him of growing up, of his parents, of a time when coming home meant love and family and people who he could truly count on. It'd been a long time since he'd felt that way, and he wasn't even sure such a thing existed anymore.

Aria was still standing in the entryway, arms crossed over her chest, watching him. "Ben, do you want to date me?"

What did she just say?

Ben could hear the blood pounding in his ears, his heart thumping in his chest. Eyes wide, he tried to open his mouth to say something...anything. Nothing came. He was barely out of a divorce from a woman who'd shredded his heart to pieces. A new job in two days. Dating...dating wasn't in the cards right now.

"I...uh, well..."

"Based on the terrified look on your face, your answer is *no*," Aria supplied for him, walking closer to the couch. "And my answer is definitely no."

"Definitely?" He was completely thrown right now, and wondering if he should be insulted, too.

"I don't want to date you," Aria repeated. "I don't want to date anyone. I've got a lot going on in my life, and I'd guess you do as well."

Ben nodded slowly.

"But..." Aria gestured between the two of them. "There's a connection here. Chemistry. Maybe insanity. I'm not sure what exactly, but I'm not a one-night stand. I'm not *easy*."

"Aria, stop." Ben extended his hand and she took it, letting him pull her closer, onto his lap, facing him. *God, she felt so good right there.* Wrapping one hand around the back of her neck, he threaded his fingers through her soft, golden hair. "There has never been a second where I thought you were easy. We're grown ass adults, not horny teenagers who can't think past tomorrow."

Aria giggled, dipping forward until her forehead was on his. Her hands pressed against his chest, twisting in his shirt. "I just don't want you to think I do this all the time...or that I've ever done something like this before."

Ben brushed his thumbs across her cheeks, holding her face in his hands. "I wouldn't be here if I didn't think *this* was something we couldn't—or shouldn't—ignore."

"Even if only for one weekend?"

"Especially if only for one weekend." Ben pulled her closer to him so that she was straddling him, her knees on either side of his waist as he sat on the couch with her on top of him. "This may not be able to go past Sunday night, but we can enjoy it now."

Her hands slid up his chest to his neck, gripping his shoulders. "Ben?"

"Yes?"

Piercing blue-gray eyes bore into his, needing and begging. He wanted to pause and press fast-forward all at once.

"Kiss me," she breathed. "Kiss me right n—"

He crushed his lips to hers before she even finished speaking, breathing in her words. She moaned against him, and Ben had to slow himself down to control his excitement. He ran his tongue across her bottom lip slowly, coaxing her mouth open. When she finally parted, he plunged inside, recapturing what he'd found so insatiable the first time they kissed.

His hands wove through her hair, pulling her as close to him as two people could be. Still, he wanted more. He wanted closer. He wanted everything.

Aria pressed her hips down, beginning to grind against him. He was already hard as a rock and the motions were dizzying. When she unclasped the top button of his jeans and slid down his zipper, he couldn't contain his groan of relief.

He sprang free into her waiting hand.

"Fuck, Aria." Ben slid his hands down her back and cupped her ass. "Keep doing that."

Her fingers circled his length, sliding up and down perfectly, while he pushed his hips up to meet her. When her head fell back ever so slightly, he took advantage of her exposed flesh, sinking his teeth into her neck. Pulling the soft skin into his mouth, he sucked, nipped, and licked his way from her jaw to the top of her breasts.

She let go of him, and before he could complain, she pulled her shirt over her head and tossed it on the floor behind them. Ben reached around and unfastened her bra, letting it fall between them.

Perfect, pink nipples stared back at him. Small, delicate, surrounded by pale full, flesh. She was a million times more beautiful than he could ever have imagined in his fantasies.

"Aria..."

"I know they're small." Her hands quickly moved to cover her breasts, a blush creeping up her face as if she was suddenly having doubts. "The last guy I was with loved to remind me how poorly endowed I am."

Unexpected rage soared through Ben's body. "Are you kidding me? Someone said that to you?"

Aria didn't reply, but the pink on her cheeks now became bright red.

"Stand up," Ben instructed, pushing both of them up and off the couch. "Where's the bedroom?"

Once standing, she pointed toward an open door across from them. "Over there. Why?"

"Because what I'm going to do to your body is going to need space." Placing a hand on either side of her waist, he lifted her up against him and she wrapped her legs around his hips. "When I'm done with you, you will never doubt again that you aren't the most beautiful woman that has ever existed."

Aria tucked her face into his neck, wrapping her arms around him. "Ben..."

"Don't argue with me on this."

She laughed, and he felt it tickle the skin on his neck. It was perfect, and happy. "I wouldn't dare."

When they reached her bed, he placed her down gently on top of the duvet. In one quick motion, he gripped his own shirt behind his neck and pulled it over his head.

Aria's eyes trailed down his body, widening as she went. Her breath quickened, and her breasts moved with each inhale.

Ben pushed his jeans down to the floor and stepped out of them, leaving him entirely naked. Reaching forward, he unfastened the top of her pants and slid them down her legs.

She was wearing a small black lace pair of panties, and nothing else. Lying back against the bedspread, she looked almost angelic. Too good to taste, and yet, that was all he wanted to do.

Ben pulled her hips to the edge of the bed and kneeled between her legs. His teeth grasped the soft lace, pulling. She shuddered beneath him, trembling and soaking the fabric.

Once he had her completely naked, he pushed her legs wider until she was entirely open for him. Glistening, waiting, Ben heard her breathe ragged, raspy pulls of air, stretched out in front of him.

"Aria, I need you to hear me." One hand on each of her knees, he slid his palms up her thighs and over her hips to her stomach.

Pushing up onto her elbows, she fixed light blue eyes on him. The usual murky gray gone, she was nearly translucent. Windows into her soul, her heart, she opened everything to him.

"You are the most beautiful woman I've ever seen, ever touched, ever dreamed of."

His hands slid over her stomach, brushing against the bottom of her breasts. She was holding her breath, focused entirely on him.

"Whoever implied otherwise, he's fucking crazy. Do you understand?" Ben waited till she nodded. "Everything about you is perfect, and I need to know you know that."

"Ben..."

He could hear the doubt in her voice, but he wasn't having it. "Aria, do you trust me?"

"Should I?"

"Logically? No." His hand slid across her skin and rested over her heart, palm flat feeling her heartbeat beneath her ribs. "But here? Yes."

She swallowed again, and he followed the wave in her throat. "I do."

"Then trust me when I say there isn't a single thing about you I would change."

Aria smiled, sitting and taking his face in her hands. She kissed him in a way that spoke, a way that told him she appreciated his honesty, his adoration. He kissed her until he wasn't sure he could stop, his mind fuzzy.

Pulling apart, he pressed her down onto the bed so she was lying on her back. Her legs spread before him, and he felt a hunger inside him that had everything to do with her. "I need to taste you, Aria."

She shivered at his words then nearly bounced off the bed when his tongue flicked over her most sensitive bundle of nerves.

"Ben!"

He dove in deeper, alternating between pushing inside her with his tongue, suckling her, and licking the length of her core. She writhed beneath him, pumping her hips against his face as she moaned and gasped with every flick of his tongue.

When she began to shake, he pushed two fingers inside her and massaged her deepest pleasure point until she began to spasm and cry out.

"Oh, God! Ben..." Aria panted, her hands twisting in the blanket beneath her and her knees clutching tight against him. "Oh, my God..."

He sucked harder until she went limp against the mattress, small moans coming from her lips. "I love how hard you come, beautiful."

Aria giggled and covered her face with her hands. "I'm not sure I ever have like that before."

Ben growled his approval, climbing onto the bed above her and pulling her farther up onto the mattress beneath him. "I like the sound of that."

He buried his face in her neck, kissing and nipping her flesh. She wrapped her legs and arms around him, softly moaning with every touch.

"I like you," she whispered so softly, he almost missed it.

But he didn't miss it, and he didn't miss how his heart soared in response. Ben gently pushed the hair off her face, and kissed her cheek and then the other. "I like you, Aria."

"Just for this weekend."

Ben chuckled. There was that sense of relief again. "Free agents."

"Ben, I can't wait any longer. I need you inside me." Aria pushed her hips against him. "Please..."

Hell. Yes.

He was already hard as a rock and had been since they began. Suddenly, he remembered he didn't have any protection with him. "Shit. I don't have a condom."

Aria blinked. "What?"

"Do you have any?"

She shook her head. "I don't think so. Oh, wait!" She scrambled out from under him and climbed off the bed. "There's a convenience store in the building. I'll be right back."

Ben fell back against the mattress, naked and throbbing. *Damn it.*

"I'm taking cash from your wallet," she said, already picking his pants up off the floor and fishing through his pockets. "It'll take me forever to find my purse in those boxes."

Ben chuckled. "Help yourself, but for god's sake, woman, *hurry!*"

"I'm going! I'm going!" She held up a twenty-dollar bill she'd fished from his wallet then yanked on his shirt and a pair of sweatpants that were hanging over a chair in the corner. "Don't lose that!"

"What?"

She pointed to his pelvis. "Him."

Ben snorted a laugh, and threw a pillow across the room at her. "WILL YOU GO ALREADY?"

"Already gone!" she called out, the front door slamming behind her.

This was quickly becoming a weekend he'd never forget.

CHAPTER SIX

A sense of eager anticipation filled Aria as she turned the knob and pushed open her apartment door. "Got the—"

A strong arm reached out and hooked around her waist.

"*Ack!*" A second arm slid beneath her knees and scooped her off the floor, and she found herself being carried toward the bedroom by a very naked, very hard, very sexy man.

She smirked, holding on to him and kicking her legs for fun. "Someone's eager..."

Ben's eyes were dark and brooding, but the grin on his face sent shivers through her body. "You took forever."

"I was gone five minutes!"

"Exactly."

Her clothes were already being pulled off in a combined effort as he lowered her onto the bed and climbed back on top. She loved every touch of his body pressing down on hers, completely covering her. His skin was fire against hers, and she never wanted to cool down.

She handed him the box she'd just purchased which he quickly ripped open, grabbing the first one he could reach. Once fully situated, Ben tossed the box on the nightstand. "We're going to need the rest of those later."

Aria's heart beat faster in her chest. "Oh."

"Problem?" He was nearly growling, brushing himself against her entrance as he kneeled between her legs.

"Only if you don't keep your promise."

He shot her a wicked grin. "God, I like you."

Aria tried to ignore the flutter in her chest. "Then fuck me."

He pressed inside of her slowly at first, letting her adjust to his width. "You feel amazing," he groaned.

She arched her back, gasping at the perfect invasion that hit each and every nerve ending in her body. Trembling, she wrapped her arms around his neck, securing herself to him, kissing his skin.

They turned feverish as he pressed in and out of her, clawing at each other like it was never enough, like they needed more. She needed more. Then he slid one hand between them, finding her clit with his thumb and rubbing circles over it until she couldn't see straight.

Stars burst and dazzled behind her eyelids. Everything was floating, fading, yet, at the same time, she'd never felt such tension building before.

"Come for me, Aria," he whispered into her ear, nibbling and kissing down her neck as he thrust harder, faster.

Lights crackled as she fell over the edge, tumbling into ecstasy as her body spasmed and shook with the weight of her orgasm. "Oh, Ben. Ben!"

"Holy shit," Ben ground out, grabbing her hips and pressing deeper than before. He froze for a moment, holding her there against him, groaning.

She ran her fingers across his arms—rigid, solid muscles. Every part of him was chiseled and defined, something she hadn't fully appreciated until she'd seen him entirely naked.

Being an actress, she often saw built men, but they were...polished? There was no mystery that they made fitness a big part of their lives, and much of their time was devoted to it. But Ben? He was rugged and natural, and while she was sure he worked out, there was also an ease to him that was comforting.

The tension finally left his body as he sagged against her, sliding to the side instead of crushing her. Exhaling loudly, he pushed off the bed and headed for the bathroom. Returning a minute later, he crawled back in to bed next to her.

"Come here." His voice was subdued, but he reached for her.

She curled into his side, drawing circles on his chest with her index finger. "Worth the five-minute wait?"

"Would have been worth a five-year wait."

Aria smiled. "I like free-agent us."

He just grunted at that, but wrapped both arms around her and pulled her to his chest. "Do free agents nap in the middle of a Saturday?"

"That's actually a requirement."

Ben laughed, and damn, she loved his laugh. It moved his whole body, rumbling inside him with such genuine spirit. It was contagious, making her heart lighter. The feeling of his chest moving against her cheek, roaring and muted all at once.

"Oh, but there is one stipulation for free agent napping," Aria added.

"What's that?"

She wiggled closer to him, wrapping her arms around his torso even though she knew the arm beneath him would probably go numb soon. "Free agents cuddle. It's mandatory."

"Good, because that's my plan for the entire weekend." Ben kissed the top of her head. "Don't let go," he mumbled around a yawn.

His breathing evened out and his muscles relaxed, and she realized he'd fallen asleep.

"I won't," she whispered.

Aria swallowed hard, trying to push down the overwhelming emotion she was feeling right now. *What on earth is my problem?* This wasn't like her. She wasn't the kind of woman who got invested in a man she'd known less than few weeks in passing, let alone have sex with him.

And yet, here she was.

There was no denying the chemistry between them, but it was more than that. An intimacy, a vulnerability...he *saw* her. When Ben looked at her, he really saw who she was. And he barely even knew her.

He made her feel adored. Worthy. Precious.

Am I being foolish? Is this just the way Ben is?

Part of her was terrified it was, and another part was terrified to find out. She wanted this to be real, even if it was only for the weekend. She wanted to feel whole and healed and being with him was already making that happen.

This had to be special to him, too. It had to.

She had never been special to anyone else.

Ben stirred. "Aria? Are you crying?" He leaned back enough to see her face.

Am I? She quickly wiped at her face, and sure enough, there were tears on her cheeks.

Ben immediately sat up and pulled her onto his lap, rubbing her back. "What's wrong, beautiful? Please talk to me."

Aria couldn't speak, a lump in her throat refused to let her. Instead, she just shook her head and buried her face in his shoulder, holding on tight. The tears continued to flow, her embarrassment rising.

He murmured sweet nothings into her ear, softly rubbing her back and cuddling her to his chest. After a few minutes, he handed her his shirt. She pulled it on, feeling instantly cradled by his scent and the soft comfort of the fabric.

"I'm sorry," she finally managed to get out. "I don't know what's wrong with me. Honestly, I have no clue why I'm crying."

"It's okay," he assured her, pulling her back down onto the bed and lifting the covers over them both. "We can lay here as long as you want."

"Thank you," she murmured, already feeling sedated from crying. Wrapped in the warm blankets and his strong arms, she drifted off to sleep feeling completely overwhelmed with everything she'd been avoiding feeling, and everything she'd been wanting to feel her whole life.

CHAPTER SEVEN

She even looks perfect when she's sleeping. And I'm completely insane. Ben tried to push the thoughts from his head, reminding himself that this was just one weekend out of his entire life. Hell, he didn't know what this was...or wasn't.

Ben lay on his side facing Aria, propped up on one elbow. He pushed a strand of hair from her cheek, tucking it behind one ear. Her chest rose and fell rhythmically as she slept, and the expression on her face was more peaceful than he'd ever seen before.

It was strange to think he'd only known this woman for a day, or that he'd only know her until tomorrow. They would return to their regular lives as strangers...coworkers...producer and actress. As if their bodies hadn't been intimately connected. As if he hadn't seen her heart pour out in tears, her vulnerability on full display.

He was still unsure what any of that had been, or what it meant. Guilt ate at him as he wondered what he'd done, or if he'd done anything at all. If it hadn't been him, then what was it that had made her cry?

Ben's body tensed, the same fierce urge he'd felt the moment he saw her tears. He wanted to protect her. Shelter her from anything and everything that could hurt her. The last time he'd felt that way...well, honestly, he couldn't remember. There'd never been a woman he'd felt such a strong sense of protectiveness over before. Certainly never so much, so quickly.

Even more strange was that Aria was probably the one woman he'd been with who didn't need his protection. She radiated strength and resilience and was clearly very independent. Yet, he'd seen her soft side. He'd seen the cracks between her tough exterior and how underneath it all, she needed affection.

Hell, everyone needed affection. He certainly did. It was part of why he was here this weekend.

"Ben?" Her eyes fluttered open. His name on her lips...it made his body pulse with warmth and excitement. "Can you stop staring at me?"

"I'm not," he lied, smiling and rolling onto his back. "You're not always the star, you know."

She snorted a laugh and whacked him softly on the chest. "Shut up."

"You did say yesterday, you're just an actress," he reminded her. That statement still stuck in his mind, saying so much more than he understood.

He wanted to ask, but he was also afraid to know.

"Really?" Aria swung her leg across his body, climbing on top of him. "Are you normally this snarky after a nap?"

That was quick. He was already rock hard against her stomach just from the sight of her bare breasts above him. Gripping her hips with his hands, he squeezed her. "This is my light snark. I'm going easy on you."

"Oh, well, *thank you*, kind sir," she replied, completely full of her own snark and sarcasm.

"Did you just call me *sir*?"

She shrugged, a wicked smile on her lips. "Problem?"

She's doing this on purpose.

"Only if you stop." In one swift move, he lifted her hips until she was directly over his length.

Aria pushed down, taking him deep inside with a soft moan. She fell forward, her palms on his bare chest. They were seared together, and for a minute, they didn't move. They just stayed like that, locked together, staring in one another's eyes.

Ben's heart raced against his ribcage, pounding harder with every second until all he could hear was his own pulse thundering throughout his entire body. Finally, the pressure was too much, the need too great. Reaching for the nightstand, he ripped open the foil packet and rolled the condom over his cock. Gripping her hips with his hands, he lifted her just enough to pull her right back down. Again and again, he thrust inside her as she bounced on top of him.

Soft pants and gasps filled the air, but no words were exchanged. There was nothing either of them needed to say in that moment. He just wanted to take her all in—the way her breasts swelled with every press of their bodies, how her eyes rolled back with each moan from her lips, the way their bodies merged, a perfect fit.

He dug his fingers into her hips as their bodies splintered and shattered. She fell forward, blond hair sweeping across his face. He wrapped his arms around her, holding her tight against his chest, loving the feeling of being so close to her.

Pushing the hair from her face, he kissing her cheeks, then her nose, and finally her forehead. She murmured something nonsensical, and it was the happiest sound he'd ever heard. Like a mixture of bliss and contentment that he felt a little proud he'd helped create.

Suddenly, a loud growling sound broke the silence.

His brow furrowed. "What was that?"

"Uh...nothing." Aria quickly sat up and reached over the edge of the bed, grabbing his shirt and putting it on. The loud growling sound happened again, and her face went beat red. "Okay, maybe it's my stomach."

Ben laughed. "Hungry?"

"I mean, we did have quite a work out," she teased.

"What are you in the mood for? I could cook us something." Ben stretched slowly, yawning. He looked around the room, but he didn't have anything to wear except his jeans since he hadn't worn boxers today and she was wearing his shirt. "You wouldn't happen to have any sweatpants that are too big for you or something like that?"

He really didn't feel like wearing scratchy denim right now.

"Um, let me check." She climbed out of bed, clad only in his shirt and a pair of panties. Rummaging around in the dresser, she suddenly paused. "Oh, these are *perfect*." She held up a large pair of sweatpants with a drawstring waist. They were neon tie-dye. Seriously, he was almost blinded by a pair of pants surely right out of the seventies. "Here you go."

Ben raised one brow. "That's all you've got?"

"Yep. They're huge. They'll fit you."

"Gee, thanks."

She laughed and tossed the pants at him. "I wasn't calling you huge, weirdo. Plus, I bet you'll look great in tie-dye."

"No one has ever looked great in tie-dye." He slid the lightweight linen pants on, securing the drawstring around his waist to keep them from falling down. *At least they're comfortable.*

Aria suddenly burst out laughing, bending forward and grabbing her knees. "Oh. My. God. You look ridiculous."

He lunged for her, pulling her against him and swatting her ass. "Brat!" he teased.

She squealed and laughed harder, wrestling away from him and running from the bedroom into the kitchen. "I'm just kidding! You look like such a stud. A very hippie stud."

"And you accused *me* of being snarky." He pushed her back against the kitchen counter and took her face in his hands, brushing his lips across hers. "You want to keep ragging on my pants, or do you want me to feed you?"

Her eyes widened, and she glanced down at his pelvis.

He burst out laughing. "I wasn't talking about my dick, Aria."

"I wouldn't hate it if you were." She flounced away from him, a teasing smile on her face as she opened the refrigerator. "But I am actually starving."

"What do you have?" He peered over her shoulder. "Eggs, bread, and...that's all you have?"

Aria pulled out both and placed them on the counter. "You should see my takeout menu drawer." Her stomach growled again, louder this time.

"I think your stomach may destroy us both if we have to wait for delivery. Guess we're having breakfast for dinner!"

She glanced up at the clock on the wall. "Holy shit, it's already dinnertime?"

He could barely believe it either. "Well, we did sleep the last few hours away." Ben began heating up the stove, placing a pan on the burner, and cutting holes in the bread to make eggs-in-a-basket.

Aria stood behind him and ran her hands up and down his back. Her warmth seeped into his skin as she leaned into him and rested her cheek against his bare shoulder blades. With a feathery touch, she slid her hands around his waist and clasped her fingers over his stomach.

His pulse flamed to life.

"I like this," she said, barely above a whisper.

Ben placed the bread in the pan and cracked eggs into the center. "Like what?"

"You. Me. Free agents." Her loud exhale fanned her breath across his skin, and a fluttering sensation built in his stomach. "It's like a mini-vacation from life."

Ben chuckled. "As if either of us even have time for a vacation."

"That's what makes it even better."

The eggs began to cook, and Ben turned around to face her. He kissed her forehead as she leaned into his chest. "It doesn't feel like we only met two weeks ago."

"Maybe we didn't."

"What do you mean?" Ben ran a hand through her hair, loving the silky feel between his fingers.

She shrugged, her cheek pressed against his chest. "Maybe we already recognized each other. Something in our souls said...*I know him.*"

Part of Ben wanted to grab his clothes and run out the door. This was intense, much more than he could handle. But he didn't move. He didn't do a thing because he wanted to know he wasn't alone in what he was feeling. They were in this together...whatever *this* was. "I thought you didn't believe in soul mates."

"I don't," she assured him. He wasn't sure whether he should be elated or hurt. "But, maybe I can buy into souls. Souls that feel a kinship when they meet someone with a similar spirit."

Ben didn't reply, stroking her hair once more before he turned back to the eggs to flip them. A minute later, he put them on a plate and handed her one.

She took hers into the living room, and it seemed only natural that he follow. As soon as he settled onto the couch, she curled against him, and they ate in silence. The eggs were a bit bland, but Ben quickly discovered he was ravenous, and the taste hardly registered.

"Ben, if I ask you something, will you promise not to judge me?" She put her empty plate down on the coffee table and turned to face him.

"Really hard to be the judging type in neon tie-dye, babe."

She laughed. "Fair point. Okay, well, since this is our mini-vacation, there's one thing I want to do."

"What's that?"

"The Walking Dead."

Ben blinked. "Excuse me?"

"I want to finish binge watching *The Walking Dead*. It's a zombie show—remember, don't judge! I'm already on the fifth season, but I have to watch it with my hands in front of my face because it's so bloody and gross and I can't handle it. But I still need to know what happens, which means I need you to tell me what's on the screen."

"Okay, I lied," Ben said, throwing his hands up.

She furrowed her brow. "About what?"

He laughed. "I'm *definitely* judging you."

Aria smacked his chest. "Rude." A crafty smile gently curved her lips. "So, will you be my eyes?"

He'd already seen all of The Walking Dead episodes because it was one of his favorites, so he certainly wouldn't mind watching it again. Plus, the way she rambled with excitement and embarrassment was so cute that there was no way he was turning down her request. "I'm game, but I have one condition."

"Anything. Well, not anything. I mean, what's your condition?"

"We order delivery. Pizza, Chinese, I don't care what. I'm fucking starving."

Aria popped up and headed back in the kitchen, returning with a giant stack of menus. Her voice lowered, sultry and sweet, as she climbed onto his lap, her legs wrapping around him. "At your service, sir."

Ben's tie-dye pants immediately felt too tight, and he groaned at the exquisite feeling of her on top of him again. "Damn it, Aria. Don't call me that when I'm trying to focus on food and zombies."

She smirked. "Yes, *sir*."

Free agents, my ass. How was he supposed to walk away at the end of this when he wasn't even sure he wanted to?

CHAPTER EIGHT

Aria's eyes flew open, her body in a cold sweat. Sitting up on the bed, she glanced around her dark bedroom. No zombies. It was just a dream.

That's the last time I binge watch The Walking Dead before bed.

Soft exhales next to her caught her attention. Ben was fast asleep on his back, one arm stretched out toward her. The fear she'd been feeling moments ago dissipated, replaced by a warmth that was becoming her norm every time she looked at him.

Two weeks she'd known the man. And yet, there was no denying there was something here. It was insane...right? She wanted to believe that it was just lust, but that didn't fit what was happening between them.

Hell, she had *cried* in front of him. And why?

She still didn't really know. Sex had never been such an emotional release for her before, but this hadn't felt like sex. It felt so much more. He'd cherished her, made her feel valued and precious. She wasn't a virgin by any means, but she'd only had sex in serious relationships she could count on one hand. Even then, not a single one of those experiences had made her feel as loved as Ben had.

Which was insane because they didn't love each other. They didn't even know each other.

So, why did it feel like they did?

Aria ran a finger across the V on his hips that pointed down under the neon tie-dye pants he was still wearing. She'd asked him yesterday if he'd wanted to date. The look on his face...he'd been horrified.

He didn't want to date her.

She *definitely* didn't want to date him.

She didn't want to be with anyone. Her career was just starting, and honestly, she was still feeling hurt and haunted by her relationship with Russell. Until the movie was released and officially done, he'd always be lurking nearby. Everything about her life right now was so unresolved and unstable.

Dating Ben Lawson was not an option.

Falling for Ben Lawson was even less of an option.

Pulling her legs underneath her, she crawled closer to him and leaned against his chest. "Ben?" she whispered, stroking the side of his face with the back of her hand. "Ben, wake up."

"Mmm," he mumbled.

"Ben," she coaxed again, this time placing soft kisses across the line of his jaw. "Wake up."

He circled her with his arms, pulling her across his warm chest. "What time is it?"

"I don't know, but I want to show you something. Get dressed."

Ben opened his eyes, his brow furrowed. "Are we going somewhere?"

"Yep!" She was already up and out of bed. Sliding his shirt off her body, she tossed it to him. A couple minutes later, he was dressed in his regular clothes from earlier and she was in leggings and a loose sweater.

"It's one in the morning." Ben pointed at the clock then looked at her like she was crazy. Maybe she was, a little. "What are we doing?"

"Going to the beach, of course." She smirked, enjoying purposefully leaving things unclear. If this was their once-in-a-lifetime weekend, their free-agent vacation, it had to include a trip to the beach.

"What!" Ben sputtered. "Is it even open? Am I going to have to get someone to bail us out of jail?"

"Santa Monica is actually one of the only beaches in Los Angeles that's open around the clock, because of the pier," she informed him, pushing him out the door and locking it behind her. "Come on. It'll be fun."

"All right, but if you need a handsome knight in shining armor to save you from beach vagrants, I charge for my services."

Aria laughed. "What's the charge?"

They reached the bottom of the stairs of her apartment complex, which opened onto the sidewalk. He immediately took her hand in his, kissing the back of her fingers. "Wild monkey sex for hours and hours."

"We weren't already doing that?" she teased.

He swatted her ass then wrapped his arm around her shoulder. "I cannot believe you have me up at one in the morning to go to the beach. I haven't done something like this in...probably a decade."

"Since college?" she asked, sliding her arm around his waist as they walked in the direction of the beach under dimly lit streetlights. "How old are you anyway?"

"I just turned thirty last month."

"Oh man, I didn't realize I was getting involved with such an old-timer," she kidded. "I'm only twenty-five. Really, you're robbing the cradle."

Ben laughed, the same deep belly laugh she loved feeling vibrate through his entire body. "Five-year difference. Wow, we're such deviants." His sarcasm was thick.

"Deviant enough to go to the beach at one in the morning."

"True." He kissed her temple and squeezed her even closer to him. "Do you do this often? The beach at night?"

"Sometimes. If I can't sleep. It can be a bit dangerous alone."

"Please don't do this alone," he quickly interrupted, gripping her tighter. His gaze turned hard, his voice strained. "Promise me, Aria. If you want to go to the beach in the middle of the night, call me first."

"I thought we were going our separate ways after this weekend..." She didn't know why she mentioned that, because honestly, she didn't want the reminder. She didn't want to hear his rejection.

He didn't say anything for a few seconds, then he let out a heavy sigh. "We are, but...just call me."

She didn't respond. Arms linked, they arrived at the beach a few minutes later and headed down onto the sand. The Santa Monica pier was to their right, but far enough down that the lights barely reached them. It was gorgeous though, and one of her favorite parts of this walk. Bright red, gold, and green lights twinkled across the wooden pier, the large Ferris wheel standing tall and casting a gorgeous shimmer over the water. It was iconic and mesmerizing, and one of the reasons why she never wanted to leave Hollywood.

Aria slipped off her sandals, and Ben carried them plus his own shoes. The sand looked black beneath her toes, the water stretching out in front of them like a mirror reflecting the stars above.

"It's really beautiful," Ben murmured as they reached the water's edge.

Beautiful barely even did it justice. The water was like glass, cast with the lights from the pier. She could stare at it for hours.

She shivered against the chill brought on by the wind over the water despite the chunky sweater she wore.

He rubbed her shoulders but looked just as cold. "I wish I had a jacket to give you. Maybe we should head back?"

She shook her head. "The walk will warm us up. Plus, you haven't seen the best part yet."

"I think I have."

When she looked at him to see what he meant, he was staring right at her with a dreamy smile on his face that made her core heat and need pulsed through her entire body. "Charmer," she teased.

"Prince Charming?" He laced his fingers with her as they walked toward the pier on the sand.

She laughed. "I definitely did *not* say that."

"That's what I heard." He shrugged. "And, I agree."

Aria rolled her eyes. "I swear, I have no idea why I like you."

"But you *do* like me, so joke's on you."

"MOVE!" A kid came barreling past them, almost knocking her over, as they got closer to the pier. "PIKACHU!"

"What the fuck?" Ben grabbed her and pulled her out of the way of several kids now running past them.

Aria just laughed. "This is the best part I was telling you about. Come on, let's get a good seat."

"Are they playing Pokémon Go?" he asked. "Not that I'd know what that is."

Aria laughed at his embarrassed tone. "Suuuure you don't."

They walked up the beach away from the water and sat down in the sand. Kids were milling around the beach under the pier and nearby, their phones in the air. They'd randomly shout out the name of a Pokémon, and other kids would rush over with their phones held high. It was exciting and fun, and absolutely ridiculous.

"This is what you like to do? Watch kids play a game on their phones?" Ben asked, his elbows on his knees.

Aria wrapped one arm around his and leaned her head against his shoulder. "Yep."

"It does look like they're having fun," he admitted. "It's certainly fun to watch. They're bumping into each other."

"Sometimes I need to remember what it's like to be so unencumbered. So free. Just innocent kids playing a silly game, and enjoying life in the moment," she explained, curling tighter into him. God, he felt so good. Just pressed against his body, his thick arms and the warmth radiating off him. She'd never been so affectionate in her life, but with Ben, she never wanted to stop touching him. "Can you even remember a time in your life where you were so free, you'd play games on a beach in the middle of the night?"

"Never," Ben admitted.

She looked up at him, her chin on his arm and a heaviness weighing on her heart. There was so much intimacy in his reply, and she wanted to take everything he was offering her and ask for more. "Never?"

His face grew cloudy, troubled. "I started working when I was a teenager. My mother didn't stick around long enough to see me take my first step. My father raised me, and he was a great man—truly wonderful—but he was tough. He worked in the industry and had me working alongside him by the time I was thirteen. I've been working ever since."

"You never got to be a kid." Aria's heart ached for him, for the loss of his innocent childhood years, and a mother's love.

He shook his head. "Waste of time, according to my pops."

"My parents would spoil you," Aria said after a few quiet moments. "They'd love all over you. I'm the oldest of three girls, and my parents are still as in love as they ever were."

"I think I saw your mother on set...was that her?"

Aria nodded. "She's my manager, so she's with me on most projects. The rest of the time, she's taking care of my father. He has multiple sclerosis, and it's pretty advanced."

"I'm sorry to hear that." Ben leaned down and moved to kiss her cheek.

Turning her face, she captured his lips with hers instead. Soft, sensual, sweet...their kiss was affection, not lust. He pulled her down onto the sand until he was stretched out next to her, his top half leaning over her as they kissed.

She ran her fingers through his dark brown hair, parting her lips as his tongue explored her mouth. They were far enough from the pier to be alone, and the lack of lights left them in near darkness. She kissed him with abandon, putting her whole heart into it.

And it hurt. It hurt so fucking much.

Because in less than twenty-four hours, it would be over.

He'd be gone.

CHAPTER NINE

I'm in so much deeper than I meant to be.

Ben wiped his hand against the mirror in Aria's bathroom, removing the steamy fog from the glass. He looked...luminous. Happy. Relaxed. He hadn't seen that on his face in years, or maybe never.

"Ben!" Aria called out from the bedroom. "I cannot pick a script. They are all so good! I need your expert opinion."

"I'm an expert now?" He grabbed a towel from the rack and wrapping it around his waist. He opened the bathroom door so that she could see him standing at the sink. "About time you admitted my brilliance."

She laughed, glancing up from the bed where she lay surrounded by a pile of paperwork — scripts, from the look of it. She was only wearing a tight, white tank top and black lace panties.

73

Fuck. She's so sexy. Ben adjusted himself, taking a deep breath. Despite all the reasons he'd just gone over in the shower about why he couldn't, wouldn't, and shouldn't date anyone right now, one look at Aria made all his excuses seem...flimsy.

"I admit nothing," she teased. "But, you've practically grown up on movie sets thanks to your father. You know this business like the back of your hand."

Ben couldn't argue with that. He'd been groomed early on to take over a company like Shepherd Films, although he'd certainly had his sights set higher than one of the oldest studios in Hollywood that was mostly floundering.

"I used to, at least." He had an uphill battle in front of him, and this was just another reminder why there was no time to add a romance to his life.

Particularly an actress who is working on one of his films. He'd already made that mistake once — and he'd married her.

Two torturous years later, his ex-wife had dragged his name through the tabloids accusing him of everything possible just to get as much of his hard-earned wealth as she could. She'd succeeded, too. He'd paid a hefty sum to end that chapter of his life, and there was no way in hell he was going to put himself in that position again.

"How was your shower?" Aria asked, smiling from the bed. That smile. He'd never seen anything like it. It seemed to reside in her eyes even more than her lips, lighting her entire face with a pure joy he could only dream of.

"Good," he replied, walking into the bedroom. "Would have been better if you were in there with me."

Aria giggled, but shook her head. "After the last thirty-six hours, I'm surprised I can still walk. Plus, I've got to go through these scripts."

"I thought this was our vacation weekend." He pulled off his towel and tossed it at her. "No work. No experts."

She batted the towel away, but there was no mistaking her eyes dipping down to his pelvis. She chewed on the edge of her lip, and damn, he nearly came at that very sight.

"I'm trying to pick my next project. So, help me, Mr. Hollywood Big Wig."

"Pick whichever pays the most," he joked, grabbing a fresh shirt and pair of boxers out of the bag of clothes he'd had delivered to her apartment earlier today. Adding a pair of sweatpants, he finished dressing and dropped onto the bed behind her, kissing her shoulder. "What are you looking at?"

"Well, there's a sci-fi movie that says I've got the role—no audition." She held up a thick script and leaned back against his chest, flipping through the pages. "I'd be playing a half-human, half-robot who learns to feel emotions by falling in love with a time-traveling alien while pregnant with a werewolf's child."

"Pass."

She glanced up at him, chuckling. "That fast?"

"I literally don't have to think about it a second longer. Hard pass."

"Okay, fair. The only thing I found redeeming about this script was that I wouldn't have to audition for it."

Ben nuzzled her neck, kissing down her shoulder. "Soon you'll be getting so many script offers you'll never need to audition again."

She made a happy murmuring sound, almost like a soft hum. "Wouldn't that be nice?"

"It's going to happen," he repeated. After seeing her on set, and knowing her background, he had no doubt.

"Okay, well what about another period piece? This one's a Victorian-type romance. The heroine falls in love with her fiancé's brother, and it destroys both of their families." Aria handed him the script.

Ben opened it up and read the first page. "It's well-written. That's a good sign."

"I'd need to audition in London this week," she explained. "I might not even get it."

He had no doubt she'd get anything she auditioned for, but the distance bothered him. It shouldn't. After all, today was their last day.

But, fuck...it bothered him.

"What else is in the pile?" He put the period piece script to the side. "Anything shooting in America?"

She picked up a thinner script. "An HBO mini-series in New York. I think I have a great shot at this. There are only two other actresses called in for it."

"The first woman to pass the bar and become a lawyer in New York City...based on a real story. Interesting. You'd do very well in it," Ben commented, reading over the front of the script. "Is there anything in the pile that shoots right here in Los Angeles?"

She let out a small laugh. "If I didn't know better, I'd think you didn't want me to leave."

He remained silent even though everything inside him screamed, *I don't.*

"There's this one," she continued. "But it's a stretch that I'd get the part. This one is going to be huge—major money backing it."

"*Scarlet's Letters* is going to be huge. You're going to be huge," he assured her. "What's this one about?"

Her face lit up as she began to speak. "It's based on a bestselling novel titled *Murals* about a famous female graffiti artist on the run from the police for the murals she creates in the middle of the night. All of her art makes political or human rights statements, and she becomes the voice of a revolution."

"Who's producing that?" His interest was immediately piqued. That script sounded fantastic. "And I vote that script."

"Because it's Los Angeles?" Aria put the script down on the bed and climbed onto his lap. "Are you trying to keep me close, Ben Lawson?"

She was a siren, brushing her lips against his jaw. Her voice low and raspy, a whispered question he didn't want to answer. He couldn't answer. The answer was too overwhelming.

"Aria..." he warned. The husk in his voice betrayed his feelings almost as much as his length pressing against her.

Her lips found his and he grasped the back of her head, pulling her to him. Devouring her lips, he pulled her down onto the mattress with him, knocking all the scripts to the ground in a flutter of papers.

"Tell me the truth," she whispered again. "Tell me you want me to stay near. Tell me this weekend meant as much to you as it meant to me."

The way she stared up at him, he couldn't lie. But he couldn't speak. He didn't know how to say what he was feeling, because he wasn't even sure himself.

"Ben, please..." she begged. "I need to know it's not just me. I'm going crazy here. We've spent two days together—that's it. I get how crazy that is. I'm not asking for a proposal or for you to profess your undying love. I swear, I'm not. I just need to know this hasn't been in my head. Are we real?"

What was he supposed to say to that? This was the most real thing he'd experienced in his entire life, but it was also ending in a matter of hours.

They'd agreed on that. They both needed that.

"Just tell me." She gripped his hips with her knees, pushing her core against him. "Please."

Ben reached down between them and gripped the hem of her black panties, pushing them down her legs. His boxers were gone next, and he pushed inside her. He had to feel her, be enveloped by her, consume her. Growling again, he sunk his teeth into her shoulder, unable to say what she wanted to hear.

She cried out, her back bowing off the bed as she pushed her hips toward him, taking every inch of him.

"I want to tell you," he whispered in her ear, thrusting into her. "I want to, but I can't. Tomorrow, we go back to strangers. We go back to...nothing. And it's going to fucking break me, Aria. It's going to break me, and I have no idea why."

Tears slid down her cheeks, and she pushed her hips against him. "I'm already breaking."

Ben pushed his arms under her back, wrapping himself entirely around her as he thrust in and out. "God, Aria."

She moaned, burying her face in his shoulder. "I'm so close, Ben."

He wasn't wearing any protection, but he wanted to feel her unravel. He *needed* to feel her unravel. At the very least, he wanted to give her this.

"Ben?" She blinked, looking up at him confused as he pulled away from her and slid down her body. The moment his tongue slid across her core, she jolted and gasped. "Oh!"

She came in seconds, slamming her hips against his mouth as he sucked and nibbled and licked until she was shouting for him to stop.

Aria gasped and moaned. "No more...I can't!"

As her climax subsided, her left soft kisses on her core and slowly traced his way up her stomach. He found her left breast, taking her nipple between his teeth. She shuddered and moaned. He cupped her other breast in his hand, squeezing her nipple between his fingers.

Aria pushed against him, turning him onto his back and climbing on top. "My turn."

He lifted one brow, waiting for her move.

She slid down his body slowly, scraping her nails down his abs and kissing his stomach. Her tongue trailed the line of his muscles as she moved south.

He could barely contain himself when she wrapped her full lips around him, taking him deep in her throat. "Damn it, Aria. Your mouth...fuck, that feels so good."

She slid her tongue around him, her fist wrapped around his base. Moving up and down, she brought him to the edge and pushed him over.

"I'm coming," he warned, trying to push her away.

She held on tighter, gripping his ass and demanding he give her everything he had. Lights exploded in front of his eyes and he burst apart inside her mouth.

Trying to catch his breath, he stared up at the ceiling. He'd had blowjobs before, but this was different. It wasn't like she was some pro or had some special tricks. It was like...they fit.

She crawled up his body, collapsing on his side with one arm and leg flung across his body.

Swallowing hard, he tried to keep his emotions at bay. But he couldn't. He just couldn't keep his heart from throbbing against his rib cage. "Aria?"

"Mmm..." She murmured sleepily against his chest, her body getting heavier as sleep began to overtake her.

"We are real. *This* is real."

She turned and kissed his chest softly. "I know."

"Tomorrow..." He swallowed again. "I'm going to miss you, Aria. I barely know you. It seems crazy..."

"It is crazy," she whispered, hugging her arm tighter around him. "Completely nuts."

Ben turned to face her, taking her chin in his hand and searching her blue-gray eyes. "Tonight might be it, but I'm not going far. I'll help you get whatever script you want. Anything you ever need in your career—just call me."

"Ben, that's not why I'm with you..."

He shook his head. "I know that. I know what this is. I know we're real." A solitary tear slid down her cheek, and he wiped it away with the pads of his thumbs. "And I know tomorrow we go back to reality. But you're a part of me now, Aria."

"Ugh...Ben!" She wrapped her arms around his neck. "Why can't we just make this work?"

Even as she said it, he could hear her doubt. He could hear that something was holding her back. Something unresolved in her life, her past. She was in the same boat he was.

Her question was as unresolved as he felt.

He wanted them. He wanted an *us*. And at the same time...he didn't. He had too much on his plate, too much on his heart. He had nothing to give another person, let alone himself.

But in that moment, he knew saying goodbye might be the biggest mistake he'd ever make.

And he'd already made it.

CHAPTER TEN

Aria opened her eyes slowly, a ray of sun shining across her face. She shielded her eyes and turned toward Ben.

Except her arm fell on the empty mattress.

She didn't get out of bed and look around. She didn't call out for him. There was no need to. She knew immediately...he was gone.

It was Monday, and their free-agent weekend was over. They were over. She hadn't expected to feel such a hole in her heart, such an emptiness in her very existence. And yet, the pain of Ben's departure was worse than any break-up she'd been through.

And they hadn't even been a couple.

It had been a fun, intimate weekend with a man she barely knew. A man she had an intense connection with, but a man whose life wasn't compatible with hers. Hell, it was a lot more than just their lives that didn't match up.

Ben was angry. His very existence was angry. His natural state of being was tenseness and frustration. She wasn't fully aware why—though she could guess his recent divorce and the stress of his new job were contributing factors.

The sweet, loving side of Ben she'd gotten to know...that probably wasn't even really him. It was just a role they were both playing in the shared fantasy that was their weekend.

All she did know was he had been very clear— he didn't want to date her. He wasn't ready to date anyone. Period.

She wasn't going to push that. There was no positive outcome for her doing that. The man she'd eventually end up with, he'd want her no matter what. No matter how. He'd want *her*.

Ben wasn't ready. And, truthfully, she wasn't either.

But for him? God, she wished she was.

Slowly, Aria pushed herself up into a sitting position, pulling the sheet around her naked body. Tears slid down her cheeks and she let them come. It was a release she needed after two days on such a high. They'd climbed to the top of the mountain and now she was falling face first into the valley.

And she was okay with that. She just needed to...she needed to get through it. Aria was nothing if not resilient.

When she felt the heaviness lift from her heart, the catharsis of her tears providing her the breather she desperately needed, Aria got out of bed and headed to the shower.

Fifteen minutes later, she was clean, dressed, and famished. Her stomach growling, she made her way into the kitchen to cook a quick breakfast before she had to head to her parent's house. She and her mother/manager — or as she referred to her lovingly, her 'momager' — needed to meet and go over the plan for her next steps.

Aria came to a halt when she saw the note on her kitchen counter. It was Ben's messy scribbles, and even though she'd only seen his writing a few times in the margins of her scripts, it was instantly recognizable.

Anything you need, call me. This was real, Aria.
-Ben

His phone number and email were scrawled at the bottom of the note. Aria ran her finger over the ink, feeling the words etched into the paper. She slid her phone from her pocket and plugged in his number and email into her contacts. There was no way in hell she was going to call him, but it couldn't hurt to keep the number.

At least, that's what she was going to tell herself.

Swallowing hard, she turned toward the stove and began prepping what she needed to poach some eggs. While those were cooking, she brewed a quick cup of coffee on her Keurig and sipped the delectable black coffee — her favorite.

Despite her job, and her desire to become famous, she happily lived a no-frills lifestyle. She liked her comfy, no-fuss apartment overlooking the beach.

The insistent peal of her cell phone broke the silence; its vibration inside her pocket bringing her back to reality. She retrieved the phone and checked the screen before answering. "Hi, Mom."

"Hey, sweet baby girl. You on your way over?" Her mother's voice was so soft and serene through the phone. Just the sound of it calmed Aria's anxieties.

"In a minute. I'm finishing up breakfast."

"Okay, well I've been looking at these scripts, and I think we should try out for all of them except the sci-fi one. It's..."

"Weird as fuck," Aria finished her sentence.

"Well, yes. That's certainly one way to put it. You never know, though. Weird movies like that sometimes hit it big."

Aria propped the phone between her shoulder and ear as she scooped her eggs from the boiling water and placed them in a bowl. "Right, but I don't want to do that. I don't want to do a movie I'm not excited about, even if it might be the next big blockbuster."

"The manager side of me finds your ethics very strict." Her mother chuckled. "But the mom side of me is super proud."

"Thanks, Mom." She took a bite of her eggs. God, that hit the spot perfectly. "So, we're deciding between the HBO mini-series in New York, or the Victorian-movie in London?"

"Or the artist movie here in Los Angeles, *Murals*. I think that might be my favorite so far, but they've got people like Jennifer Lawrence and Natalie Portman coming in to audition for that."

"So, there's no chance I'd get that role."

"Aria Marie Reynolds, I did *not* raise you to be a quitter. You're just as good as any of those ladies."

"Mom..." Aria began to argue, because there was no way she was in the same league as either of those actresses — though she certainly wished she was.

"No arguments, Aria. There's always ways to make it happen. With a lot of practice, you could give the performance of a lifetime in that audition and they'd hire you on the spot. Or, we could offer to take less money. Budget always talks in movies, you know. We could also call your cousin. I'm sure he'd put a good word in for you after his success in that new silly superhero movie."

"That movie was not silly," Aria countered. "And we're *not* calling him. I'm doing this on my own. I don't want his help."

"Fine, but as your manager, I think we should be utilizing all the connections we can find."

Aria's mind drifted to Ben as she finished the last of her eggs. She had no doubt if she called him up and asked to star in the studio's next film, he'd make it happen. Just like she had no doubt if she called her cousin, he'd catapult her career. But that's exactly why she didn't go by her last name in the public eye.

Aria Rose was her way of earning it for herself, and on her own merit. That might be foolish in the cutthroat world of Hollywood, but she was determined to do it anyways.

"I'll be over soon, Mom. Let's get auditions set up for New York and London, and if you can get the L.A. one."

"On it, baby girl. Drive safe."

"Love you, Mom," Aria said before hanging up the phone.

Five minutes later, Aria was closing her front door behind her. As she locked it, a wave of sadness washed through her, clutching at her chest. Her apartment had been a cozy retreat for the weekend with a fantasy man, and closing the door made it all seem so final.

They were over.

I'm being ridiculous. She shook her head and took the stairs down two at a time, got in her car, and headed to her parent's house.

"Aria!" Simone, her baby sister, greeted her with a hug the moment she walked into their parent's house. "You look different. Why do you look different?"

"I do?" Aria furrowed her brows.

"You do. Tegan, doesn't she look different?" Simone turned to their other sister, the middle daughter. She was only two years younger than Aria. Simone was the baby of the family, and a senior in high school, while Tegan was working as a choreographer and dancer in Hollywood—also with the help of their mother.

"She looks..." Tegan tapped her chin with an index finger. "Oh, shit. You got some, didn't you?"

Warmth crept into Aria's face. "Tegan!"

Tegan laughed and draped an arm around Simone's shoulder. "That look, little sister, is the look of a woman who had really good sex last night."

"Gross." Simone scrunched up her face.

"Jesus, Tegan. She's too young to hear things about my sex life," Aria scolded her sister. "Not appropriate."

Tegan just shrugged. "Fuck, I was doing worse at seventeen than hearing about sex."

"Anyway," Aria tried to steer the conversation away. "Where are the parentals?" she asked, using the nickname the sisters used for their parents.

"Dad's watching television in the living room. Mom's at the dining room table with an insane amount of scripts," Simone said, walking toward the living room.

Aria followed her, smiling the moment she spotted her father. He was propped up in a big, comfy recliner watching Storage Wars—a television show about pawnshops and storage unit auctions that he was obsessed with.

She leaned down to give him a kiss on the cheek. "Hi, Daddy!"

"Hey, princess," he replied, then pointed at the television. "Look at that lamp. He's trying to sell it for four hundred dollars, saying it's centuries old...but it's electric. Idiot scammers. They don't know who they're messing with!"

"Sounds intense." Aria watched for a moment with him, then squeezed his shoulder. "I'm going to go find Mom. You doing okay? Can I get you anything?"

"I'm right as rain, princess. Your mom takes great care of me." His multiple sclerosis had stolen most of his ability to walk, and he needed a lot of help getting around.

Aria hated seeing him so dependent and disabled, but his spirit never seemed to be affected by any of it. He was still the lively, loving father she'd grown up with, and for that, she was really appreciative.

"Aria?" her mother called out.

She headed for the dining room. "Hey, Mom."

"Hi, sweet girl." She kissed her on the cheek when Aria bent down to hug her. "Check this out." She turned her laptop for Aria to read.

"I got the audition?" Aria gasped. "For the HBO show?"

"Yep. And I've booked you on a flight for New York City tomorrow. You'll audition Wednesday, and fly to London on Thursday. You're auditioning for the Victorian movie on Friday. Next week, you're back in Los Angeles for a crap ton of photo shoots for *Scarlet's Letters* promotion."

"But, I've got to memorize the lines and practice! That's not enough time!" Aria began to feel panicked and nauseous. Auditions were terrifying—they always had been.

"Relax, sweetheart. You'll do just fine. You've got two days and a lot of time on planes to memorize everything. You're a natural."

Aria nodded, trying to push down her fear as a queasiness threatened to overtake her. She'd felt the same nervous flutter in her stomach before her *Scarlet's Letters* audition, too. Actually, she had vomited right beforehand in a trash can outside the studio, and was certain she'd pass out the moment she stepped on stage. Luckily, she'd aced the role instead, but it didn't get less scary with each new venture. "Any word on *Murals*?"

Her mother shook her head. "Not yet, but I just got an email that Jennifer Lawrence is officially in talks for it."

Aria's body sagged. She felt crushed. She'd been looking at all these scripts for weeks, trying to narrow it down, and she'd told herself that she'd be fine with any of them. And yet, the news that *Murals* wasn't happening bothered her more than she thought it would. "Damn. I really loved that script."

"I know, honey. I'm sorry. I'll keep tabs on it, though. You never know."

She sighed, sitting in the chair next to her mother. "So...New York?"

"Here." Her mother handed her the HBO script. "Read it over and then we can run lines in a few hours."

Aria turned to the first page and took a deep breath. She could do this. In fact, it was exciting. She *would* be excited about this. Her career was moving along, and she was more than ready to launch herself into Hollywood stardom.

CHAPTER ELEVEN

"The writing is terrible," Ben argued. "There's no way in hell this studio is picking it up."

Arthur Atwood sat across the desk from him, his hands folded in his lap. "Okay, well, that's all we've got at the moment. So, do you have any bright ideas?"

Ben sat back in his office chair, thinking it over. "I know I've only been here two days, Arthur. I get that, but I'm here because we need to take Shepherd Films in a new direction. We need quality scripts, and the writing is everything. It's make or break it."

"I agree, but the best scripts come with the largest price tags. You've seen the company budget. We're in the red until *Scarlet's Letters* comes out, and we're banking on that hitting big."

"*Scarlet's Letters* is going to be huge. I have no doubt." Ben stood from his desk and began pacing the room. "We need new talent. Talent that doesn't have a huge price tag yet, who we can pay in gross points on the backend."

Arthur thought it over for a few minutes, and Ben kept pacing.

"I do know of one new writer who's been getting some buzz," Arthur finally said, clapping his hands. "He won a few independent film writers awards, recently graduated New York University. We could always go meet with him, see if he'll write something for us. Or what he's already got written."

"Schedule it. I want to meet with him tomorrow," Ben instructed Arthur, then walked out of his office to where his assistant was sitting. "Jackson, book Arthur and I two tickets to New York City tonight. Hotel reservations through Thursday, as well."

"Yes, sir," the young man said, already clicking away on his computer.

"And don't use company funds. I'll pay for it." Ben handed the man his credit card. Overhead costs needed to be cut fast or people would have to be let go from their jobs — something Ben wasn't willing to do. He'd much rather shoulder some of the financial burden himself.

Ben had spent most of Monday catching up on everything he needed to know about the company, and today he'd wanted to hit the ground running. He still had a lot to learn about Shepherd Films, but they couldn't afford to wait for him to study every detail. He'd learn as he went, and had Arthur to help him in the meantime.

"Jackson's booking us a flight and hotel," Ben informed Arthur as he walked back into the office.

Arthur nodded. "Good. Trying to reach the writer now."

A few hours later, he and Arthur were seated first class on their way to New York. Arthur was in the row behind him and already asleep and snoring very loudly, even though they'd only taken off a few minutes ago.

Ben sighed and leaned his head back against the headrest. Murmuring at the front of the cabin began to grate on his nerves. He had Arthur kicking the back of his seat, and flight attendants excitedly chatting in front of him. So much for a nap.

A small smile spread across his face. Naps would forever make him think of Aria now. He couldn't help it. Leaving her apartment Monday morning had been one of the worst moments of his life. Sleeping in his own bed last night...torture.

It had never felt so empty before. *He'd* never felt so empty before.

"Aria Rose is back there!" The flight attendant spoke just loud enough for him to catch what she was saying.

Ben's eyes flew open. *Aria?*

"No!" The other flight attendant looked thrilled. "She's on the plane? Why is she in coach?"

"I don't know," whispered the first flight attendant. "Maybe we should move her up?"

Ben reached above him and clicked the call button. A ring sounded and the flight attendants immediately stood up straighter. The first one smoothed her skirt, plastered on a smile and walked over to him.

"Good afternoon, sir. Can I get you something?"

Ben pulled out his wallet, handing over a credit card. "I'd like to upgrade Ms. Rose's ticket to first class. This seat here." He gestured to the empty one next to him.

"Certainly, sir." She looked elated, taking the card. "I'll let her know immediately."

"Thank you," he replied. His heart was already pounding in his chest. They'd only been apart two days, and now they were on the same flight? He wasn't sure what it meant, or if it was some type of sign, but he sure as hell wasn't about to ignore it.

"Ben Lawson. Are you stalking me now?" Aria appeared at the end of his row, one hand on her hip and a devilish smile on her lips. She was wearing dark jeans under tall, leather boots with an oversized cable-knit sweater and wide-brimmed hat. Despite her attempt to hide as much of herself as possible — probably from the paparazzi — he had no trouble remembering exactly what was hiding underneath those layers.

Ben stood and took her carry-on bag from her other hand. He opened the overhead storage and carefully slid her bag in next to his, latching it closed. "If I was, I'm certainly not doing a great job hiding it."

She stood there for a moment, staring at him, not taking the bait. The dreamy gaze in her blue-gray eyes was sultry and magnetic, as if she saw he was hiding behind humor instead of saying what he really wanted to say. Finally, she tilted her head to the side and smiled wide. "It's good to see you again, Ben."

He slid his tongue across his lower lip. "It's good to see you, too, Aria."

Her cheeks bloomed with a light blush, but she tilted her chin up. "Can I have the window seat?" she asked.

Ben chuckled. He loved her forwardness. "Whatever you'd like."

She batted long lashes at him, swinging her long blond hair over her shoulder. "I like that motto."

They both sat side-by-side, her at the window and him in the aisle seat. She took off her hat, tucking it into the pocket of the seat in front of her. "So, Ben, why are you going to New York? Aside from badly stalking me?"

"Meeting a new writer about a script," he replied. "I'm guessing you're going for the HBO script audition?"

"I am."

"So...didn't want to stay in Los Angeles?" Fuck, he hated how much he hated the idea of her living across the country.

Her lips twitched. "They're in talks with a different actress for that role."

"Too bad." And he meant it. He made a mental note to call the studio and demand they audition Aria. They'd be idiots not to.

"No. Ben, no." She raised her index finger and shook her head. "I see your mind working. Do *not* interfere."

"Who, me?" Ben put a hand to his chest, his best shocked expression on his face. "I would never do that."

She wasn't buying it. "Ben, I'm being serious. Don't."

He sighed loudly, dropping his shoulders. "Fine. If you change your mind, let me know."

"I won't."

He shrugged. "We'll see."

"Hey, Ben?" She reached over and squeezed his forearm. "Thanks for the seat upgrade. I've never been in first class before."

He didn't reply, just placed his hand over hers.

She leaned back in her seat, closing her eyes. "Would you hate me if I got some rest instead of chatting? I'm pretty tired today. Been practicing for these auditions the last two days nonstop."

"Auditions? Plural?"

"New York and London." She yawned, tilting her head toward him. Her eyes drifted closed as she placed her head on his shoulder, sending a thrill through his body.

"I've missed taking naps with you," he whispered into her ear, brushing a lock of hair from her face.

Aria giggled and cuddled into him tighter. "Free agent flight?"

"I could live with that."

She tilted up to look at him, and he pressed his lips to hers. Gentle, soft kisses that were pure affection and enjoyment. It was different from their usual frenzied passion, but felt as intimate, if not more. He slid his tongue across her lips and she opened for him, lifting her hand to his face to cup his cheek.

They stayed like that for minutes. Soft, slow kisses. His body ached for her, but he didn't push further. He could have suggested they meet up in the bathroom and join the mile-high club, or get a blanket and fool around underneath, but he didn't.

He couldn't. It was hard enough walking away two days ago. If he had her again now, there was no way he'd say goodbye again.

But kissing her? He wasn't strong enough *not* to do that.

"Oh, Ben..." Her breathy whisper slid past her lips after several minutes. "What are we doing?"

"Mmm." He tilted his forehead toward hers, their breath mixing together. "I don't know, Aria. I don't fucking know."

He was surprised at how strained his words sounded. Pained. Aching. Everything he felt inside leaking out.

"It's a long flight," he finally said. "Let's just take that nap."

She nodded, her face a strange mixture of disappointment and relief. "Okay."

Ben pushed up the armrest between them, and she curled in to his side with her head on his chest. He wrapped his arm tight around her, trying to memorize exactly how she felt.

He hadn't done enough of that this weekend. He'd loved their time together, and dreaded it ending, but he hadn't prepared himself for what it would be like after she was gone. He hadn't memorized the warmth of her skin, the curve of her neck when she lay against him, or the gentle smell of vanilla when he pressed his face to her hair.

He wasn't going to forget a thing this time.

Aria slid her hand into his, intertwining their fingers. "Wake me when we get to New York?"

"Of course." He kissed the top of her head. "Get some rest, movie star."

She chuckled sleepily. "Sure thing, Mr. Big Shot."

Ben had been on an airplane dozens of times, but this was the first flight he hoped never landed. He could stay floating in the clouds with Aria pressed against him forever.

CHAPTER TWELVE

Aria ran her fingers through her hair, staring at her reflection in the hotel mirror. Silently, she mouthed her audition lines as she grabbed her mascara tube and pulled out the wand. Applying a few more coats to her lashes, she tried to bury the nerves fluttering in her stomach.

"You've got this, Aria Marie Reynolds," she muttered to herself. "You've got this."

Her cell phone rang from the counter top, and she clicked it on to speaker while she applied a bit more blush to her cheeks. "Hello?"

"Aria, have you been online today?" Her mother's voice sounded frantic.

"What?" She furrowed her brows and picked up a tube of lipstick next. "No. Why?"

"Someone on your flight yesterday snapped a picture of you."

Aria froze. *With Ben.*

"With your boyfriend," her mother continued. "All cuddled up and kissing him. The internet is ablaze with trying to figure out who is Aria Rose's mystery man."

"Shit." Aria sighed and picked up the phone, turning off the speaker and holding it up to her ear. She remembered one of the flight attendants with her phone out giving her furtive glances, and guessed she'd probably been the leak. "Mom, I can explain."

"Good, because I'd love to know why the paparazzi knows about your love life before your own mother. Who is this man and why has he not come over for dinner?"

Aria chuckled lightly. "He's not my boyfriend. We're not dating."

"Well, if he lives in Los Angeles, I expect him over for dinner soon."

"Not happening, Mom."

"Wasn't asking, Aria. Anyway, leave early for your audition because you might have some paparazzi issues in the lobby. They already know where you're staying."

Aria groaned. "Crap. I need to leave now then. I'll call you after the audition. Thanks for the heads up, Mom."

"Love you, baby. Kill them dead out there."

She rolled her eyes. "Yes, Mother."

After hanging up the phone, she tossed it into her clutch along with her hotel key card. A wide-brimmed hat and giant sunglasses later, she was ready to go.

Stepping onto the elevator, she continued going over her lines in her head. This role was exciting, and she wanted to knock it out of the park. *Murals* had been her top choice, but the HBO show was her second choice and she wanted it just as badly. Aria stepped into the lobby after the elevator doors opened.

A frenzied-looking hotel clerk came rushing over to her. "Miss Rose?"

She offered him a wide smile. "Yes?"

"We've arranged for you to go out a side entrance." He gestured toward a hallway leading away from the main doors.

Aria frowned and looked to the revolving door that she'd entered last night. Lights began flashing, hands banged against the glass, and the shouting sounded like a dull roar.

"ARIA ROSE! ARIA ROSE! WHO ARE YOU DATING?"

"TELL US HIS NAME!"

"ARE YOU GETTING MARRIED?"

"IS THIS A STUNT FOR YOUR UPCOMING MOVIE?"

"ARE YOU IN LOVE?"

There were only about a dozen photographers, and yet, they had all the persistence and volume of a giant crowd.

Aria stepped back, her hand to her chest. "What the..."

"Please, miss. Follow me," the clerk said, pointing again to the back entrance.

Tears stung her eyes as she quickly followed him. It was all so overwhelming, and she didn't know what to make of the situation. She'd never been followed by paparazzi before. A photo sold here or there, sure, but actual interest in her and her life? Never.

If anything, her biggest following had always been on social media. Photos she chose and shared with her fans. She loved the control of it, the ability to share herself with the world but in a way that still made her feel safe and comfortable. Her strength in marketing her image on those sites had really catapulted her career—apparently more than she'd even realized.

The clerk graciously showed her through a side entrance and into a waiting car service. "Please give us a call on your way back, and we'll make sure to have the side cleared for you to enter."

"Thank you. I will."

"Where are we headed, Miss Rose?" the driver called from the front seat.

Aria gave him the address and sat back in her seat. Her hands were shaking as she replayed all the things the reporters had been shouting. Opening her clutch while still trembling, she pulled at her phone and called the only person she could think of.

"Aria?" he answered the phone on the second ring.

"Ben..." Her voice caught, and she sniffed, trying to find her calm. "Have you seen the news?"

"I just did. Are you okay?"

"The hotel...a dozen photographers...everyone was shouting at me. I've never—Ben, I've never...I would never call them. You know I didn't do this, right?"

"Aria, I have no doubt you weren't involved. It was probably that flight attendant who kept staring at us. But, seriously, are you okay? You sound really worked up."

"Of course I'm worked up, Ben." Aria tossed her hand up in the air in frustration. "My photos are all over the internet. Photographers know what hotel I'm at. This isn't my life...this isn't who I am. I'm a private person."

Ben chuckled, and it irritated the crap out of her. "You're probably going to have a lot more of that in the years to come. Your career is on the rise."

Aria groaned, rubbing a hand to her face. "What if people figure out who the *mystery man* in the photo is? Ben, they're going to think..."

"They're not going to find out. I saw the photos and your hand is on my face in the majority of them. It's pretty hard to make out who it is."

"Really?" That was good news, at least. She couldn't have her relationship with Ben getting out there.

He'd be considered the stud who bagged the up-and-coming actress, but she'd be called the slut sleeping her way to the best roles.

"And even if they did find out, I'd never let them print a bad word about you." His voice lowered, almost husky. "You know that, right?"

She nodded, even though he couldn't see her. "Promise?"

"Yes. It'll all be okay," he assured her.

His voice was so soothing that she felt herself calming down. This wasn't the end of the world. It was just a sign of her career flourishing.

It was a good thing. Right?

"I guess I just got really flustered by the attention. I like my privacy, and I definitely didn't like all the photographers out there yelling at me. The assumptions...I just don't want to be in the tabloids."

"Understandable," he replied gently. "But also, a hazard of the profession."

"I know. Sorry for calling," she said softly into the phone. "I know we said—"

"Don't ever be sorry for calling, Aria," he interrupted. "I'm here whenever you need me."

She was quiet for a moment, just enjoying hearing the sound of his breathing on the other end. "Goodbye, Ben."

"Goodbye, Aria."

She hung up the phone and tucked it back into her clutch. They were almost to her destination, and she had to concentrate on her audition. She didn't have time to worry about what the internet was saying about her, or her *mystery man*.

CHAPTER THIRTEEN

"Hey, Ben!" Arthur Atwood appeared in Ben's office doorway. "The deal is done. We've got the kid!"

"Great," Ben replied, leaning back in his chair. "We've got the script. Time to narrow down a list of directors. Let's get Creative Artists Agency on the phone. They represent half of Hollywood."

"Good idea." Arthur sat in the chair across his desk and started scrolling through his phone. "Although, we could always use Russell Rains again. He liked working with us, and he's great at what he does."

Ben nodded, considering it. "He is a great director, but...let's just see what other options are out there."

There was no doubt that Rains was one of the best, but Ben got an uneasy vibe from him sometimes. Rains was a notorious playboy, and everyone knew his penchant for a dramatic love life. Ben wasn't opposed to working with him again, but wanted to keep his options open.

His phone beeped from his pocket. He pulled it out and glanced at the screen, excitement coursing through him to see Aria's name over the text. He opened it up—a photograph—and let out a laugh.

She was obviously in London, leaning forward and pretending to kiss the air, but the Big Ben clock tower was in the background so it looked like she was kissing the clock. Her text underneath read "I've always wanted to kiss Big Ben in London."

He quickly typed up a reply. *He'd like that, too.*

She answered almost immediately. *A girl can dream.*

"Who are you texting?" Arthur asked. "You look like a Catholic school girl over there giggling."

Heat flooded Ben's face, and he put away his phone. "Nobody. Did you get CAA on the line?"

"Working on it," Arthur replied. "But, I'm not stupid, you know."

Ben furrowed his brow. "Did I say...?"

"Our lead actress is all over the tabloids this week about a mystery romance on a flight to New York. You're over here texting like my teenage daughter on her way to prom. I can put two and two together."

Damn. Ben had thought he was safe since most of the photos only showed the back of his face, or a sliver of the side. Aria was the one more prominently featured, unfortunately. Arthur was definitely smart. Ben was glad to have him on his team.

"We're not dating," Ben clarified. "But yes, I'm the mystery guy in the papers."

"That's even worse." Arthur groaned, rubbing a hand across his face. "You don't have real feelings for her, but you're willing to risk both of your careers for a roll in the sheets? Fuck, if you're hard up, I know a massage parlor that—"

"Arthur, I'm fine," Ben interrupted him. "We're all adults. It's not a big deal."

"For you personally, maybe not. For the company and for her career? It's a huge fucking deal. We're trying to bring Shepherd Films back to the main stage, and you're going to make us look like a side show act if people think we cast based on who will sleep with the boss."

"That's not what happened at all and you know it," Ben said, his tone angry and deep.

"It doesn't matter what I know. It matters how it'll look to the press."

"Fine. We'll talk to public relations. Figure out how to spin it." Ben certainly didn't want to do anything that would jeopardize Aria's career. He didn't want other studios or producers thinking she slept her way to the top, because nothing was further from the truth. Hell, if she wanted to curry favors and get ahead, she'd use her real last name and her cousin's connections. But she didn't want any of that.

She wanted it on her own merit, and he wasn't going to be the one to mess it up for her.

Glancing back at his phone and her unanswered text message, he deleted their conversation. They needed to stick with the original plan. It was one weekend. And then one plane ride.

But it was over.

CHAPTER FOURTEEN

Turning to his computer, Ben clicked on the website link for Entertainment News. He needed to be up to date on the latest gossip around Hollywood, particularly when considering casting and people for this new film.

They had a director lined up now, and it wasn't Russell Rains. It was a new kid with a lot of heat behind him. Shepherd Films was trying to appeal to the millennial generation, so he'd decided to cast only the newest talent on the scene to be part of the movie.

The buzz about it was doing great so far, and if *Scarlet's Letters* turned out to be a hit, he was fairly confident he could restore Shepherd Films to its former glory.

Actress Aria Rose Cast as Lead in HBO Mini-Series About First Woman to Pass Bar Exam in New York, Katherine Stoneman.

She was the very first article that popped out on him from the page. Ben was proud of her accomplishment. Aria had the talent to play a suffragette, and she certainly had the old-school Hollywood look to play a woman in the late 1800s.

He read the article fully then leaned back from his desk, resting his head against the back of his chair. Last time he'd seen Aria was on the plane on the way to that audition. If he didn't count the picture she sent him from London a few days later.

The last month had been all work, and he was loving every minute of it. He'd thought being assigned to a dead-end studio was a demotion, but he was fast learning that it was one of the most exciting challenges of his life.

The problem wasn't the job, however. It was going home. A glass house with a view of the Hollywood sign. Beautiful modern architecture and clean lines. Most people would envy him, and he knew he should be grateful for the life he was able to live.

But all those clean lines of glass and metal was cold and unforgiving when the only occupant was him and the memories a failed marriage.

He missed the quaint coziness of Aria's apartment overlooking the beach. If he was being honest with himself, plain and simple, he missed her.

She hadn't contacted him since London, apparently busy filming the HBO series. Heat had died down slightly about her *mystery man*, but the Public Relations Department's strategy of "say nothing and it will go away" was definitely not working.

Ben reached the bottom of the article and saw another one with her name, letting out a long sign.

Actress Aria Rose Spotted Dining in New York City with Mystery Boyfriend,

Ben's teeth clenched together, and he tried to identify what he was feeling. His stomach turned because he knew for a fact that this mystery man sighting was not him. *Is she dating someone?*

Ben copied the link and sent it to her in an email with the subject line. "Need to Talk."

Fuck. I shouldn't have done that. He immediately regretted sending the email, but it was already gone.

About two minutes later, his cell rang and Aria's picture popped up on the screen.

"Hello," he answered.

"'Need to talk.'" She repeated his words, sounding slightly off put. "That's a bit rude, don't you think?"

"It got you to call," he teased.

"Ben."

He took a deep breath. "Fine. You're right—it was rude."

"Thank you." There was silence over the line for a minute. "I'm not dating anyone, if that's what you're wondering."

Ben immediately let out a long breath he hadn't even realized he was holding.

"It was dinner with Travis." Her co-star on *Scarlet's Letters*—Ben liked him. "He was in New York and wanted to catch up."

"That's nice of him."

"He actually had an interesting proposition..." Aria paused again. "It might solve some of our PR issues."

"Really?" Ben was happy for any solution at this point. He was hours away from firing the entire Public Relations Department on his end, since it shouldn't be so difficult to squash one damn story. "What's his idea?"

"Travis is—and I'm only telling you this because he gave me permission, but it needs to stay between us, promise?"

"Okay," Ben agreed, feeling wary about where this was going.

"Travis is gay, and he's not ready to come out. His family is...let's just say, not understanding." Aria sighed, and she sounded so sad that he wished he could reach through the phone and hug her. "He wants to be my Mystery Man."

Ben furrowed his brow. "Wait...what? He wants you to be his beard?"

"Yeah, and I'm totally fine with that if it will help him. He was so distraught, Ben. We need to do this for him."

Ben chuckled quietly, unable to keep the smile from his face. God, he loved how kind she was, how much she always did to help others. After thinking it over for a moment, he gripped the phone a little tighter. "You know, this might actually work out well. Tabloid stories about co-stars dating can do wonders for movie promotions. *Scarlet's Letters* would definitely be helped by it. Travis would get to keep his secret a little while longer—though I wish he didn't feel like he has to. And you and I..."

"We will be a distant secret long over that no one needs to find out about," she finished for him. "No more rumors circulating about my love life, and no possibility of people thinking I slept my way into a role."

Distant secret. She wasn't wrong, of course, but it was hard to hear. He was beginning to wonder how distant he really wanted them to be.

"I want to meet with both you and Travis to plan this. Can you fly to Los Angeles soon?"

"I'm still filming the mini-series for 2 more weeks, and then I'm coming back to audition for *Murals*," Aria explained. "We could meet then."

"*Murals*? I thought you said they were in talks with someone else."

"They were, but it fell through. Looks like I may get a shot!" Aria sounded excited, and he could almost visualize her doing a little dance at the very idea of it.

"That's fantastic. HBO and big box office. Told you that you were going place. I'll send you and Travis a meeting request via email. See you then?"

"Sounds good." Aria's voice got a little quieter, trailing off. "Goodbye, Ben."

"Goodbye, Aria."

He hung up the phone and looked at the calendar. Two weeks and she'd be standing in front of him again. There was no doubt he'd count down every day until then, and he hated himself for his lack of control. She was not his girlfriend, and she didn't want to be. Hell, he didn't want her to be.

Time to stop thinking with his heart and get back to being in charge. He was cutthroat in the boardroom and the studio, and one weekend of lust — love — wasn't going to change that.

CHAPTER FIFTEEN

Hearing his voice was hard. So damn hard.

Aria stared at her phone after she hung up the call with Ben. Walking over to the hotel window, she looked out at Manhattan below her. Gray. Dark. Desolate.

New York had once been her favorite place to visit, but the last few weeks of filming hadn't been enough of a distraction to keep her from thinking of him.

Everything was such a mess now. The one man she wanted could tank her career. So, she was choosing her career over him, and she hated how sad that made her feel. She hated that she couldn't have both in a world where women were judged harshly by who they dated.

Her phone rang again, and her heart leapt in her chest to talk to Ben again. "Hello?" she answered quickly, without looking.

"Hey, baby girl," her mother's voice came across the line. "Listen, I got your voice message about Travis and I think it's absolutely nuts. Your father does, too. Here, see?"

"IT'S NUTS!" he shouted in the background, and Aria guessed her mother had held up the phone to him.

"Mom..."

"But," her mother continued, speaking over her. "I think you might be right. I think this will lead to a lot of good press for the movie. Co-stars dating is a paparazzi's wet dream."

"Mom. Gross."

"Well, it's the truth." Aria head a muffled sound on the phone and then her mother returned, her voice lowered now. "But, that still doesn't explain to me — your goddamn mother — who your mystery man is."

"I told you. It was a one-time thing."

"Aria, I swear to God, you're going to tell me eventually."

"I'm not," Aria replied in a singsong tone.

"You are." Her mother matched her tune. "But enough of how you're trying to break your mother's heart and send her into an early grave, did you get the script for the L.A. movie?"

"*Murals*? I did. I'm going to start practicing tonight."

"Good. Jennifer Lawrence turned it down — signed on to a movie with Chris Pratt instead," her mother explained.

"And I'm next up?" Aria sometimes couldn't believe her life. The fact that she was even having these kinds of conversations was mind-blowing...and ego-inflating.

"Well, a few other people turned it down, too. And you're a lot cheaper than them, so we've got a good shop."

Ego down. Aria rolled her eyes. Her mother always knew how to put her back in her place. "Thanks, Mom."

"No need for sarcasm, Aria. Study those lines. I'll see you when you get back—two weeks, right?"

"Yep. It's going to be jam-packed. The audition, *Scarlet's Letters* promo photo shoot, meeting with Shepherd Film studio exec, the Travis situation..."

"You're going to be even busier when *Scarlet's Letters* wins an Oscar and you're the hottest actress in Hollywood!"

"Mom..."

"Don't argue with me, Aria. And drink some water. You don't drink enough water."

"Okay, Mom. Love you."

"Love you, too, baby girl." Her mother hung up the phone.

Aria tossed her cell phone onto the unmade hotel bed then collapsed onto the sheets next to it. She missed her own bed. Her own apartment. She missed the man she'd last shared it with.

Aria sighed. Things were beginning to feel way too complicated, and yet, at the same time, so simple.

She missed Ben. And she wished that she didn't.

CHAPTER SIXTEEN

"Ready, *baby*?" Travis exaggerated the nickname as he took Aria's hand while they walked across the airport terminal.

She took a deep breath. "You know there are going to be a million reporters the moment we step out of the airport, right?"

Travis furrowed his brow. "Are you nervous? We don't have to do this, Aria. You're doing me a *huge* favor, but I'd never want to make you uncomfortable."

"No, I'm doing this." She readjusted her bag on her shoulder. "I just hate paparazzi. Tabloids. All of it. It's such an invasion."

"I kind of like it," Travis admitted, squeezing her hand tighter. "I'd rather they want me, than not know I exist."

He had a point. Fame was a double-edged sword.

"Travis, can you promise me one thing?" she asked as they neared the exit.

"Anything."

"One day—when you're ready—tell the world the truth. You're one of the best guys I know, and any man would be lucky to have you."

Travis smiled and gave her a sideways hug. "I love you, kid."

"Love you, too." And the truth was, she did. Travis had been working on a new independent movie in New York City at the same time as she'd been filming the HBO series—not to mention all the time they'd spent as lovers and co-stars in *Scarlet's Letters*—and they'd spent a lot of time together as friends when they weren't on set. She absolutely adored his sweet nature and giving heart, and one day, she hoped the rest of the world could see what she did.

"TRAVIS PETERS! TELL US HOW YOU AND ARIA MET?"

"ARIA, WHAT'S IT LIKE FILMING A SCENE WITH YOUR BOYFRIEND?"

"ARE YOU GUYS IN LOVE?"

"ANY PLANS TO WALK DOWN THE AISLE SOON?"

Microphones were shoved in their faces the moment they stepped out onto the sidewalk, and the shouted questions continued, though the words quickly blended into a dull roar. A burly security guard was already pushing photographers out of the way and guiding Aria and Travis to a waiting car. Her hand never left Travis', holding tighter as the crowd swarmed them from either side.

"Jesus Christ!" Travis gasped as the collapsed on the back seat of the town car with tinted windows, the door slamming shut behind them. "That was insane!"

He was smiling, but Aria was nearly shaking. "Insane," she repeated, her voice trembling.

"Are you okay?" Travis pushed closer to her on the seat and wrapped an arm around her. "Damn, you're shaking like a leaf. Aria, maybe we shouldn't do this. It's too much."

"It's already done," she reminded him, trying her best to calm herself down. The crowds, the pushing, the shoving, the screaming. She felt silly that it bothered her so much, but it was frightening. Despite her rising fame, she tried to live as quiet a life as possible — until now, apparently. "They already got pictures of us holding hands and flying together. Mystery Man revealed."

Travis sat back and sighed. "I'm sorry, Aria. I never should have roped you into this."

"Travis, stop." She put a hand up. "I'm just being a wimp. I'm an introvert, you know? I'm more than happy to do this for you."

He surveyed her face as if he was trying to see if she was lying. She just stared at him harder. Finally, he nodded. "Okay. Well, thank you. Again."

Forty-five minutes of Los Angeles traffic later, they arrived at Shepherd Film Studios and headed straight for Ben's office.

"Hi, Jackson," Aria greeted Ben's assistant who was sitting at a large desk outside of Ben's office.

He smiled brightly up at them, his eyes lingering a little longer on Travis. "Good to see you again, Miss Rose. I'll let Ben know you and Mr. Peters are here."

"He's *cute!*" Travis whispered to her the moment Jackson disappeared from the room.

Aria batted his arm. "He'll hear you! Plus, you're my boyfriend — remember?"

Jackson emerged from the office seconds later, and Travis offered Aria a sideways smirk. She stifled her laughter, nudging Travis instead.

Ben emerged from the office right behind his assistant.

The moment Aria saw him — perfectly coifed in a three-button suit that was clearly tailored for his body — every lustful memory came flooding back to her. And it wasn't just the heat in her core as she remembered how he felt pressed against her, but the flutter in her chest as she remembered how he made her smile, laugh, and feel adored and cherished.

Ben gestured for them to follow him. "Hey, guys. Come on in."

"Thanks, Mr. Lawson. It's good to see you." Travis shook his hand, then headed in first.

Aria paused in the doorway for a moment, lingering next to him. She lowered her voice and looked up at him from under long lashes. "Hi, Ben."

"Good morning, Miss Rose." He gave her a polite smile and escorted her into the office.

What the actual fuck is happening right now? Aria's brow furrowed as she tried to decipher Ben's brush off. Was he just putting on a show for Travis and Jackson? She doubted they would have noticed anything from just a secretive smile, or tiny touch of her arm.

She swallowed hard. It bothered her how much this bothered her. How upset she was that he hadn't flirted with her, touched her, or acted like they were anything other than producer and actress. Because this is exactly what she'd told him she wanted.

So...I guess this is good, she decided, mentally trying to comfort herself as she and Travis took seats across from Ben at his desk.

Ben folded his hands on the wooden desk in front of him, a picture of professionalism. "How did it go at the airport? We tipped off every photographer in town."

"Fantastic," Travis replied, his tone obviously excited. "We were nearly swarmed. Good call on the bodyguard, though. Aria was pretty freaked out."

"Are you okay?" Ben turned to her, a worried expression on his face. But, it wasn't Ben-and-Aria worried...it was co-worker-worried and she hated it.

"I'm fine." She kept her teeth clenched, her lips tight.

There was no way she was going to explain herself. He most definitely should know how much she hated being in the tabloids or swarmed by paparazzi. He'd been the first person she called when her dating life started popping up in magazines. She was not enjoying this distant side of Ben. It felt...callous.

They were closer than this. Even without the romance, they were...friends. He was acting like he barely knew her.

"All right. Glad it went well," Ben continued. "We've got the photo shoot in two days, and we're going to arrange for some fake candid photos of the two of you from the set to be leaked to the press. With only three months until the release of the movie, this will be a nice way to keep people talking about it. Closer to release we'll have you do a press tour on talk shows, radio, things like that. You should be finished filming the mini-series by then, Aria, but we'll happily work around your schedule. People will certainly be asking questions about you two by that time, so it's up to you how long you want to make this fake relationship last. Two co-stars in love sells well, but so does feuding co-stars who just broke up. We can discuss closer to date."

"Sounds good to me," Travis said, turning to her. "Aria?"

"Good with me, too."

"Jackson has some paperwork for you both to sign, and then we'll see you in a couple days for photos. We'll need you to be seen occasionally in public, and turn down any requests for interviews. Feign a need for privacy."

"I actually *do* like my privacy," Aria reminded Ben, struggling to hide the angry tone in her voice.

Ben shrugged. "Right. Well...that's Hollywood for you."

Fuck. You. Ben Lawson. Aria was nearly seeing red at this point. Did he seriously not give a shit about her? It had been about a month and a half since their weekend together, which, in the grand scheme of things, wasn't that long. Had their connection been completely in her head?

"Well, it was good meeting with you, Mr. Lawson," Travis said, sticking out his hand to shake Ben's. "We'll go get on that paperwork."

Ben stood and shook his hand, a friendly smile on his face. "Good to see you again, too, Travis."

Aria didn't say anything, just gave Ben a curt nod and headed for the door. She saw a brief flash of confusion when she didn't accept his handshake, which only made her more annoyed. It couldn't possibly be a secret to him that he was acting like an asshole.

Travis caught up to her in the hall outside his office after they'd both picked up their paperwork. "Hoooooly shit. *Aria!*"

"What?" She looked at him with alarm.

"He's the mystery man?" Travis nodded his head back toward Ben's office. "You're dating the CEO of the entire studio?"

"Really?" A familiar grating voice caught Aria off guard, and she jumped. Russell Rains stood in the hallway behind her, a sinister grin on his face. "Not such an innocent flower, are you now?"

Travis smiled at Russell. "Hey, Russ! How's it going?"

The men hugged, but Russell never took his eyes off her. Aria didn't blame Travis. He had no idea that she'd dated Russell, or that she'd thought she loved him. Or that he'd been making her life hell ever since she broke up with him. Hell, even Ben didn't know that. It wasn't exactly a proud moment in her life that she wanted to share.

"How are you, Aria?" Russell moved to hug her next, but she shrunk back, offering him a curt nod as well.

"I'm fine, Russ. Thanks."

"Oh, hey, listen, Russ," Travis began. "What you heard about Aria and Mr. Lawson? That's got to stay between us. Aria and I are pretending for the press that we're a couple."

Russell nodded. "Smart. Good publicity in co-star romance."

"Great." Travis smiled. "So, you won't say anything."

"I won't say a thing." Russell smiled again, and it looked even more wicked than before.

Aria hated that he knew anything about her, but especially this. What she had with Ben...or what she'd thought she had with him...it was none of his Goddamn business.

"See you kids on the photo shoot," Russell called out as he headed down the hallway toward Ben's office.

Aria crossed her fingers, hoping Russell really would keep his word and say nothing.

"Okay, Aria. We're doing lunch." Travis linked his arm with hers as they exited. "Because I need to know every detail of you and that hunk of man upstairs. My God, he is gorgeous."

Aria laughed, her cheeks heating as she pictured Ben's chiseled, naked body. *No, Aria. Not happening.* She pushed the images from her mind.

Ben Lawson didn't want her. Good.

Damn it.

CHAPTER SEVENTEEN

Aria stared at the stucco ceiling of her small bedroom. It was way past midnight, but she couldn't sleep. Luckily, she had all of tomorrow off and could sleep as late as she wanted. She always had the day before a photo shoot off for that reason specifically. No photographer wanted her showing up with tired eyes. Her audition for *Murals* was in a week and she really wanted that movie. Every free minute of the last few weeks had been dedicated to practicing and studying the role.

Though none of that was the reason for her sleeplessness.

The ceiling lit up and her cell phone buzzed on the nightstand. Aria rolled over and caught it before it vibrated its way onto the floor.

Are you awake?

Ben. Unbelievable.

Aria shook her head as she tried to decide what to do. She had no idea what she even wanted to hear from him. The last month and a half had been confusing, and today had only made things worse.

Sighing, she finally typed back a simple *yes*.

The phone buzzed again almost immediately. *Good. Open your door.*

Aria's eyes widened and she looked in the direction of her front door. He was here? She jumped out of bed, tossing her phone back on the nightstand. Scurrying around her room, she put away some clothes, straightened the bed, and cleaned up a dirty mug she'd had hot tea out of earlier.

On her way to the door, she glanced in the full-length mirror. Damn it. Her hair was unkempt and messy, her face washed clean with no makeup, and she was wearing an old T-shirt with holes in it. Nothing else.

Note to self: buy real pajamas. Actually, just buy lingerie. Wait, no. Don't buy lingerie, because you don't want Ben.

She ran her hands across her face, hating that she was so conflicted.

There was a soft knock on her front door, and she unlocked it, swinging it open slowly.

Ben stood in front of her, his hands in his pockets. Crap, he looked insanely good. Even better than earlier today. He was wearing the same suit, but his face was scruffy and rugged, his hair slightly mussed. His eyes darkened the moment they reached hers, his nostrils flaring, and a wave of heat flushed through her body directly to her core.

"Ben—"

He reached for her and his hands grasped her shoulders, tugging her against his taut body before she could say another word. Aria's breath stalled in her lungs. As he slid his arms around to her back, she glanced up and he crushed his lips to hers in a heated kiss. There was nothing left to do but melt into his touch—and damn, did she melt. His hands beneath her butt, he lifted her against him and she wrapped her legs around his waist as he walked them both inside.

Her mind was swimming, dizzy with the sudden ache between her legs and need swelling inside her. She pushed her hips against him, wanting to quench her desire.

Ben growled against her neck, nipping her flesh as he pushed her against the wall and closed the door behind them.

What am I doing? The lust-filled fog began to lift, and she slapped him on his chest. Pushing him away, she righted herself and readjusted her clothes. "Ben! Stop! What the hell."

He wiped his thumb across his bottom lip, grinning playfully at her. "I obviously upset you today somehow. I wanted to apologize."

"*That* is not how you apologize."

"I don't know," he teased, his eyes twinkling. "You were very...forgiving."

Aria huffed, but couldn't really argue that point. She'd been completely ready to have sex with him right there in the entry of her apartment. *Damn his rugged good looks and deep, growly voice.* "I could have been sleeping you know. It's after midnight. I am *not* a booty call, if that's what you're expecting."

"Wow. Claws out tonight, huh?" He raised a brow as he looked at her.

Aria's shoulders sagged. "I'm sorry. I'm feeling very...I don't know what I'm feeling. And you're really not helping with that." She ushered him into the living room. "Come on in. Let me take your coat."

"Thanks." He handed her his jacket then rolled up the sleeves of his button-up shirt. He settled down into the couch, patting the cushion next to him. "Join me."

Aria nibbled on the corner of her lip, debating the proximity. She was already feeling distracted by the way he was looking at her bare legs. Finally, she relented and curled up on the seat next to him, tucking her legs underneath her as if she was almost curling into herself. Tension spread throughout her body, nerves fluttering in her belly.

They stared at each other for a moment. Aria's mind was reeling, unable to focus on a single thought, but rather jumping from one to another in rapid succession. This was unfamiliar ground for her.

She'd been in relationships before, but no one had ever made her feel the way she felt when Ben was around. Weightless. Thrilling. Impulsive and exciting. He gave her the confidence to push boundaries, to step over the lines she'd spent a lifetime slave to. When he looked at her, it was limitless and anything she'd ever wanted was suddenly within reach. She hadn't even known such a feeling was possible actually, or that she'd ever felt so limited before.

That's the thing about building walls around one's heart—it's easy to forget they're there until someone begins chipping away at them.

Relationships had always been somewhat transactional for Aria before. Someone to spend time with, care for...it had always been about the other person and what role she *should* play. What they needed from her, and how she could give to them.

Ben was someone she *shouldn't* be with. No doubt about it. And yet, she was beginning to realize he was what she wanted more than anything. She wanted to take back everything she'd ever said about free agents. She *wanted* strings attached—every damn string.

Ben reached out a hand and pushed a lock of hair from her face. As his cool fingers brushed against her heated face, she nearly forgot how to breathe.

"God, I've missed you." He spoke so quietly, she almost missed it, but the admission both thrilled her at the same time that it terrified her. She was completely in this—head-over-damn-heels—and he only saw her as a fling, at best.

"Ben...don't." She shook her head and looked away, as if the answer to everything she didn't understand was somewhere in her apartment and she just needed to find it. "What are you doing here?"

"I stayed at the office all day today, and all I could think about was you, Aria. Seeing you this morning..." He was the one shaking his head now. "I don't know what I'm doing here either."

"You acted like you barely knew me today."

A frown creased his forehead. "Is that why you were so upset?"

"I wasn't upset," she shot back. *Lying. Great way to start, Aria.* "I mean, I was just confused."

"About?"

She tossed her arms up and shrugged. "I get that we're not dating. I get that we don't want anyone knowing about our..." She waved one hand between them. "...whatever this is. Was. Is? I don't know. But, we are at least friends, right?"

He nodded, his frown deepening.

"Well, you spoke to me like we were just colleagues. If even that." She was getting more worked up with every sentence, and the unshed tears burning her eyes were getting harder to hold back.

"Aria..." Ben reached for her, pulling her onto his lap and wrapping his arms around her. "I'm so sorry. I was trying to be respectful of your wishes. Keep any suspicions at bay. I do *not* think of you as a colleague. Hell, I definitely don't think of you as just a friend either."

She sniffed, tucking her head into his neck and inhaling the familiar scent of his cologne. Sandalwood and earthiness. Rugged and brusque. She couldn't get enough.

"What are we doing, Ben?" she whispered, pushing past the lump in her throat.

He groaned. Frustrated. Pained. He was visibly aching, and she was right there with him. "We're being idiots."

"You came all the way over here in the middle of the night to call me an idiot?" she asked, scrunching up her face and letting out a small chuckle. That certainly wasn't where she'd expected their conversation to go. "Gee, thanks."

Ben laughed and placed two fingers beneath her chin, tilting her face to his. "We're idiots because we're fighting *this*. Fighting us."

Aria's entire body began to tremble, her heart thumping so loud in her chest that she could hear it in her ears. She slid her tongue across her lower lip, swallowing hard. "What are you saying, Ben?"

"The free agent weekend was a stupid idea. I'm sorry, but it was. We're *not* colleagues. We're *not* friends. We're...we're—" Ben paused then shook his head. "Fuck it."

His lips were on hers in seconds. Aria's body exploded with heat as he wrapped his arms around her back and pulled her so tight to his chest, she could barely breathe.

She didn't care. She didn't want to breathe. She'd happily die pressed against his lips and pretending this was her forever—that *he* was her forever.

He pulled her bottom lip between his, nibbling the soft flesh before letting go and kissing her top lip. She parted her mouth, and his tongue dove in. They devoured each other with such fervor, such need, that she was already on the edge of orgasm just from grinding against his lap.

"Bedroom," she said, gasping for air when they came apart. "Now."

He growled, his eyes fiery and eager, then scooped her up in his arms. They continued to lock lips while he carried her to the bedroom. Laying her down on the bed, he then pulled his shirt over his head and tossed it across the room.

Aria was already wiggling out of hers, completely nude underneath except for a small pair of beige panties that she really wished she hadn't chosen to wear tonight.

"Fuck, Aria." His eyes roamed her nearly naked body as he pushed back and unbuttoned his pants, stepping out of them. "Beautiful. Just like I remembered."

"It's only been a month," she breathed, squirming on the bed because surely any moment her body would erupt in flames. He was as chiseled as she remembered, and his manhood was full and wanting before her. Her body pulsed in anticipation, her sex clenching with eagerness.

"It's been longer than that." He gripped the top hem of her panties and slid them down her legs in one quick motion. When she spread her legs, he groaned again and almost melted forward onto the bed. "Too fucking long."

"Please, I can't wait," she begged, gripping his biceps and pulling him toward her.

He pressed his body over hers, pinning her to the mattress. Making his way down her neck, he placed soft kisses over her skin before reaching down and grabbing her knees. He pushed them apart, bending them around his waist.

She clutched her knees to his hips as he pressed against her entrance. With one long thrust, he completely filled her and she gasped at the shock of his size. She wasn't sure she'd ever get used to him, but she didn't regret a thing.

"Jesus, Aria...you're so tight." His lips were to her ears as he began thrusting in and out of her. "So damn perfect."

Aria wrapped her arms around his neck, pulling her to him and kissing him with such fierceness, she almost felt dizzy. "Harder," she gasped. She wanted more. She wanted everything. She wanted to feel his strength, his power, his command. She wanted him to take her — claim her.

He slammed against her — faster and with more force than before. "I don't want to be free-agents, Aria." His words were choppy, between breaths, as he plunged in and out of her. "I want you. I need you."

Tears slid down the sides of her face at his confession. She tightened her grip on him, and kissed his neck. Bringing her lips to his ears, she whispered, "I'm yours. I always have been."

He pulled back just enough to look at her — eyes wide. She wondered if he had actually been worried she'd say no. As if there was any world where she wasn't completely wrapped around his finger.

"This is real?" he asked, an ache in his voice that shattered her completely.

"We're so fucking real," she replied just as her body began unraveling around him, waves of pleasure shooting through her as her back arched off the bed.

He held her tight to his body, waiting for her to subside, then quickly pulled out and finished on her lower abdomen. "Fuck. We need to buy more condoms."

"Or I can just go on the pill?" she offered. Feeling him inside her like that? There's no way she could go back. "I'm clean."

"I'm clean, too." He raised a brow, a mischievous grin spreading across his face. "And I like your idea. A lot."

"I'll call for an appointment in the morning," she called out to his retreating back as he headed for the bathroom.

Aria already felt exhaustion creeping over her. An hour earlier, sleep had seemed impossible and now she was struggling to keep her eyes open.

When Ben returned a minute later, a warm, wet cloth was in his hand. He gently cleaned her then returned with it to the bathroom.

She curled into the sheets, her eyes drifting closed until he crawled under the covers behind her and wrapped his arm around her waist. "I've missed this bed."

"Mmm," Aria moaned, pushing her body back against him, wanting to feel every inch of his body pressed against her. "I've never seen *your* house, you know."

"We can spend tomorrow night there if you want. I have to warn you, though. It's nowhere near as cozy as yours."

"Tomorrow night?" A smile spread over her lips. They were making plans.

"And the next night, and the night after that, and the night after that..." He trailed off, kissing her neck instead. "I want you in all my nights, Aria."

"What about your days?" she asked, because that was going to be a lot more complicated. They still couldn't be an official public, or make their relationship common knowledge. "What are we, Ben?"

He paused, quiet for a moment. "I know what I want us to be. I want it to be you and me, together. Exclusive. I want to go on dates and send you flowers and hold your hand in public."

Aria's heart soared, but reality quickly pulled it down. "But we can't. Not until after the movie is released."

She'd already agreed to help Travis, and their rumored dating was really helping the movie promotion. Not to mention the hit her reputation would take if her love life went public — dating the director, her co-star, and the producer? Really hard to come back from that mudslide.

"It's only a few more months. We could keep the secret until then."

Aria giggled, kind of liking the sound of that. "A secret romance."

"From the press, at least." Ben cuddled her tighter to him. "We could tell friends and family."

"My mother wants you to come over for dinner," Aria told him, remembering her mother's demand.

"I'd love to."

Aria heard him yawning behind her, and she yawned next. "Will you be here in the morning?"

"I'm going to be mysteriously sick from work tomorrow," he mumbled into the pillow. "I'll have to stay in bed all day."

"That's unfortunate," she teased. "I can nurse you back to health."

"God, yes."

Aria closed her eyes, lifting his hand from her waist up to her face and curling into it. They were as wrapped around each other as two people could possibly be, and she was more than ready to spend every night like this.

If she could be patient for a few more months, he could be her forever.

CHAPTER EIGHTEEN

"We can't drive in together," Aria admonished him. "How obvious would that be?"

Ben laughed and tossed a balled-up pair of socks across the room at her. "You're taking this secret romance thing very seriously, huh?"

She batted away his fabric missile with ease. "And you're acting like we should be shouting it from the rooftops."

Ben crossed the bedroom and took her in his arms. Kissing her cheeks and then her forehead, he sighed. "It does kind of suck. It's only been a day, but I feel like I could stay in this bed with you for years."

Aria murmured softly against his chest. "I know. You can't call out sick two days in a row though, and I'm not sure my body can handle another full day sex-a-thon."

"Never know until we try," he teased.

Yesterday had been one of the best days of his life, maybe almost as good as their weekend together. He'd called out of work, and they'd spent the day in bed with delivery food and sex.

A lot of sex.

Damn it, he wanted her again now even though they'd just had a quickie in the shower while getting ready for the day. "Shit, Aria. You might be my drug. I can't get enough of you."

She twisted away from him with a flirty smile. "You're crazy."

No argument here.

They quickly finished getting dressed and headed down to their separate cars. He'd go to the office as usual, and she had the photo shoot for the movie promos.

"Are you going to stop by the shoot today?" she asked, leaning over the top of her open car door.

"Maybe." He stepped closer to her, his hands in his pockets. "Tell me you want me to."

He wasn't asking, and he liked the way her eyes darkened and her cheeks flushed when he did so. She'd resist it, but she loved when he was commanding, and he loved that about her.

Aria shrugged, but the corners of her lips were tilted north. "I wouldn't hate seeing you."

"And tonight?" he asked, not taking her bait. "I'll text you the address to my place, and meet you there when you're done with the shoot."

"I might be able to pencil you into my calendar."

Ben kissed her goodbye, chuckling against her lips at her continued attempt to act nonchalant.

"You better, baby." *I love you.* The words almost tumbled out of his mouth, but he held them back, shocked at how natural the urge to say it felt. "See you later," he said instead.

She looked hesitant for a moment, then nodded. "See you at work, *boss.*"

Ben laughed and headed for his car parked a few spots away. Climbing into the driver's seat, he took a moment to take in a deep breath. The hole he'd been feeling in his life for months, maybe years, was gone. Even the brief period of time he'd been married to his ex, he'd never felt like this. He'd never felt complete.

With Aria, he felt whole. He felt invincible. She had so quickly become everything to him, fit perfectly into every part of his heart, and he'd do anything he could to keep her there. It was absolutely risky and insane, considering how quickly he'd fallen for her, but that didn't diminish the truth.

When Ben finally arrived at work, a few people asked about his absence the day before, but he feigned a stomach bug because people didn't tend to ask follow-up questions of those things. The morning went by quickly as he attempted to catch up on the work he'd missed from the day before.

He was just starting to think about lunch when his office phone rang.

"Hello?" he answered.

"Hey, baby," the familiar croon of his ex-wife came over the line.

Ben's jaw clenched, his fuse already shortening at the very idea of having to talk to a woman who'd hurt him so viciously. "What do you need, Marion?"

Needing something was the only reason she ever called nowadays.

"Need?" She feigned hurt, but he didn't buy it for a second. "Oh, Benny, come on. Can't a lady just call to catch up with her former lover?"

"Former *husband*," he corrected. "Never was that much love between us."

"Hurtful," she continued. "But not entirely wrong. We had a good thing going back then. You've got to admit both of our careers flourished together—the eternally sexy diva with her hot, young playboy. We were quite a pair in this industry."

"Until you tore us both down with that tabloid shit storm." Of course, the takeaway from their marriage for her would be about business. Everything was a transaction to get what she wanted.

"A woman scorned, Benny...you know the saying."

Ben's jaw clenched tighter. "Right." Her lack of remorse was unsettling. He'd done nothing to deserve her wrath, except not love her. "Making me look like an idiot kid who fell for a-Mrs. Robinson-type didn't work in either of our favors, Marion."

Marion sighed through the line. "Benny, can we have lunch? I'd really love to see you and catch up. Talk about more...pleasant...topics."

Shit. If she wanted to meet up, then she needed something big. Probably money. He'd already paid a hefty sum in the divorce that she easily could have lived off for years, and yet, nothing was ever enough for her. He may have been portrayed as the cougar's boy toy in the media back then, but he had always been the real breadwinner and brains of the operation.

Thankfully, he was older now and no one mistook him for a boyish nobody anymore. He'd worked hard to cut his ties in the press with Marion, and was finally beginning to be judged for his own merits. "I'm busy, Marion. I've got a new job and can't be taking lunch breaks right now."

"I heard. Head of Shepherd Films... congratulations, Benny." Her voice softened even further, almost lilting with overt sexuality. What was her angle? "I also heard you have a new film casting soon."

Ah, there it was.

He rolled his eyes, letting out a long exhale. "And you want me to cast you? Is that why you're calling?"

She huffed. "Benny, I'm insulted. I would never ask for favors. You know how seriously I take my craft."

What a load of bullshit. She'd only ever starred in B-List movies, and was now on reality television shows regularly. Not that there was anything wrong with that, but in Marion's glory days, she'd been rumored to be the next big thing. Her shitty attitude and diva behavior ended that almost before it began—not to mention their divorce splashed across Page Six making both of them look like a big joke in their May-December romance gone south.

"I'm not in charge of casting, Marion." *Not entirely a lie.*

"Benny, I just need an audition. I can earn it on my own. I know you can get me that, right?" she crooned, and his stomach turned at her desperation.

"The answer is no, Marion. Goodbye." With that, he hung up the phone.

Ben scrolled through his phone and pulled up his texts to Aria. *How's the shoot going?* he typed out.

She didn't answer right away, which made sense if she was busy, but still left him antsy. Clicking on the intercom, he buzzed his assistant. "Jackson, can you order me a couple sandwiches for lunch?"

"Sure, Mr. Lawson!" Jackson replied, ever the eager employee. "Should I use the card on file?"

"Yeah. Feel free to get yourself lunch on the order, too."

"Thank you!"

Ben clicked the intercom off and sat back, sighing. He felt...unsettled. Which was odd since that morning had been such a high. All of yesterday had been, actually. Still, something felt...off. Ominous.

And it wasn't just the phone call with Marion, though that certainly had his guard up.

It all just felt too...easy. He was too happy. A feeling he wasn't accustomed to.

Ben realized how ridiculous that sounded. On paper, he *should* be happy. He had always enjoyed success, wealth, and an easy life. But it had been so empty.

His mother had died when he was young, and he barely remembered her. His father was always working and just had him tag along when he couldn't find someone else to pawn him off on. He'd filled his youth with dates and brief flings, and when he thought he should get married, he'd settled down with the next relationship that came along.

But it had all been superficial. It had *looked* good on a glossy magazine spread, but deep down, under the silence and lonely nights, none of it was what it seemed.

"Mr. Lawson?" The intercom buzzed. "Sandwiches are here!"

That was quick. Ben stood from his office chair and put on his suit jacket, adjusting the lapels. It had only been a few hours since he'd last seen Aria, but damn, he missed her, and he was eager to get down to the shoot for lunch to see her.

CHAPTER NINETEEN

"That's perfect!" the photographer shouted to her and Travis. "More pouting, Aria."

They were posed in front of a green screen, looking longingly into each other's eyes and wearing their costumes from the movie. She pursed her lips a bit more, trying to capture the look he was asking for. This photograph would be the backdrop for the movie posters and a few others used for promotional purposes.

Travis smirked at her for a moment, then returned his composure. It was hard to stay so serious and one of them usually broke character and laughed if it went on too long.

"I think we got the shot!" the photographer confirmed a minute later after looking at his screen. "Lunch break?"

"God, yes," Aria said, letting go of Travis and shaking out her stiff limbs. Long poses made her cramp like crazy. She made a mental note to start working out more often to increase her strength. "My stomach is growling."

"I know. I could barely keep a straight face listening to that," Travis teased her. "Want to go grab lunch?"

"I think I'll meet up with..." she trailed off, realizing she probably shouldn't be saying Ben's name out loud with an entire camera crew around.

Travis nodded knowingly, a big smile on his face. "Ah, yes. Get it, girl."

Aria felt her cheeks heat, but she laughed. "You always make everything sound dirty."

He shrugged. "Best way to be."

"Hi, excuse me?" A middle-aged woman with silky brown hair walked up to the two of them just as they were walking off the shoot. She looked late-thirties, maybe early-forties, and very pretty. Aria was sure she'd seen her somewhere before.

"Hi. Can I help you?" Aria replied with a friendly smile, trying to place the woman's face.

"Yes. I'm looking for Russell Rains, the director?"

Travis pointed to the other side of the set. "That's him over there, talking to the photographer."

Another reason Aria was grateful for the lunch break. Being on set all day with Russell monitoring was not her idea of fun. At all.

"Thank you so much." The woman began to head that direction, then paused mid-step and turned back to them. "I've seen you two in the papers before, right?"

"Um...probably." Aria never knew what to say to that. Fame was a bit...embarrassing sometimes. "I'm Aria Rose. This is Travis Peters."

"Yes! I thought so! You two look as in love as the papers say." She gave them a huge smile. "Hold on to it. Love is so precious."

Travis wrapped an arm around Aria's shoulder. "I do love the heck out of this woman."

Aria just smiled, trying not to laugh. She wasn't wrong. Aria definitely loved Travis, but only as a friend.

"I'm on my way to meet with my husband after a quick chat with Russ. We've...we've had some disagreements lately, but we're going to make it work." The woman had a dreamy smile on her face and Aria suddenly placed where she knew this woman from.

Ben's ex! Wait...she didn't say ex.

Aria had seen Marion Lawson on television a few times, and her name came up in the entertainment news occasionally. It still surprised her a bit that Ben had been seriously involved with someone so much older than him, but she certainly wasn't in a position to judge someone's past relationship choices. "Oh, you're...you're visiting your husband?"

"Yep. We're having lunch. Well, thanks for indulging me. Have a great day, you two lovebirds!" Marion gave them a small wave and headed in the direction of the shoot they'd just left.

"That was weird," Travis commented, his arm still around her shoulders. "But, hey, we're better actors than we thought!"

"That's Ben's ex!" Aria hissed to him. "I mean...he *said* he was divorced."

Travis' eyes widened. "Drama! Either he lied, or she's nuts on a cracker. Personally, I'd lean toward nuts, because I'm fairly certain I saw the news of their divorce in the tabloids last year."

"For his sake, I hope so." Aria couldn't tell if she was hurt or angry, but the rage in her stomach made her lean to the latter. "I swear to God, if he lied to me, I'm going to jail for what I'll do to him."

"I'll help you hide the body," Travis offered. "Make it look like an accident? Or a disappearance? We'll never get caught!"

Aria laughed. "I love how willing you are to help me commit a felony."

"Hey, I'd do anything for the woman I love. That's just the kind of boyfriend I am."

Aria wrapped an arm around his waist, laughing harder. "Come on, let's go find some food before I get too 'hangry.'"

"I can fix that." Ben walked on to set just in time to catch the tail end of their conversation. He held up a bag of what looked like sandwiches. "Got enough for everyone."

Travis paused, looking between her and Ben. "Can I take his sandwich even though we hate him right now? I'm, like, really hungry."

Ben scooped out a sandwich and handed it to Travis. "Here you go, but why do you two hate me right now?"

Aria crossed her arms over his chest. "There's someone on set to see you."

"I'm going to eat this...somewhere else." Travis held up the sandwich. "Thanks, Ben. Catch you later, Aria."

Aria gave him a small wave, appreciating how he knew she needed the privacy.

Ben held out a sandwich to her, but she didn't take it. *Damn it. I am hungry.* No, she was sticking to her guns. Explanation first.

"Who's here to see me?" he asked, looking annoyingly perplexed.

"Your *wife*. Apparently, you two are working out your problems and staying together. Oh, and you're having lunch with her?"

Even as the words came out of her mouth, they sounded implausible. She just couldn't believe he'd lie to her, or that he was still married. He'd told her how public the divorce had been, at least until it was buried beneath the next Hollywood scandal. *Could it be possible it was never finalized?*

"Marion is here?" Ben furrowed his brow, looking around the room 'til he spotted her. "Damn it. I told her no."

"Wait, so you're not even denying you're getting back together with your wife?" Aria's eyes widened and she reached out to smack him in the chest. "What the fuck, Ben?"

"What? No, we're definitely divorced and staying that way. I'll show you the papers if you want. Signed, sealed, done. She's fucking crazy if she thinks anything else. This is clearly a stunt to try and get me to cast her in something, but nothing is going on between us, and I am *not* having lunch with her." Ben grabbed Aria's arm before she could pull away, bringing her closer to him. His voice turned quieter, gravelly and sexy. "I'm having lunch with you. And dinner with you. And hopefully dessert with you, too."

Aria exhaled a short burst, contemplating his explanation. Honestly, she believed him. Marion did have the reputation of being a few crayons short of a full box, and if she was as power-hungry as people said, then it would make sense she'd use her previous relationship to try and get into a studio.

Christ, what are the chances that we'd both have crazy exes? Aria was just glad the two didn't know each other because a Russell-Marion team sounded disastrous for everyone involved.

Sighing again, Aria pulled away enough to maintain a professional looking distance to anyone watching. "Well...you're going to need to go tell your wife that lunch is off."

Ben chuckled and shook his head. "Happily. Like I said, she is only here to try and convince me to cast her in our next film. Not going to happen."

"I'll meet you in your office?" Aria asked, letting her hand brush down the front of his suit discreetly. God, he was firm as a rock under his clothes. Maybe she was hungry for something besides just a sandwich...

"Sure, I'll be there in a second." Ben handed her the bag of food and then stalked off in the direction of his ex-wife.

Aria scurried to the exit, but then lingered, surreptitiously watching the exchange between them. Ben looked angry and was clearly being very firm with her. Marion was rolling her eyes and pouting but didn't seem to disagree with him.

Crazy bitch. There had to be something seriously wrong with someone who would just make up random lies to strangers they meet.

Having seen enough, Aria headed down the hallway and into the stairwell.

"Hey, sexy." Russell was coming up the stairs just as she was headed down. "You did great on set today."

Teeth clenched, she tried to just walk right past him. "Thanks."

"Not so fast," Russell said, placing his hand on the wall so that his outstretched arm blocked her path. "What's the hurry? We used to have fun in these stairwells, remember?"

"Russ, stop. I'm not playing this game with you."

"What's the matter? I wasn't a big enough name for you so you decided to start fucking the studio head?" Russell laughed. "I always wondered how someone from the D-List got the lead in *Scarlet's Letters.* Now I know it's because you're fucking your way to the top."

Aria recoiled as if she'd just been physically slapped. "That's not what happened and you know it."

"Do I?" Russell beamed a sinister smile. "Not sure that I do. Some free career advice, though? Stick with your fake Travis love story and dump the studio exec. *Scarlet's Letters* can't afford to tank just because our lead is a slut."

"Fuck you, Russell," Aria seethed through clench teeth. She shoved his arm out of her way and stormed past down the stairs, trying to ignore his cackling laughter above her.

"If you need to get off that badly, I'll fuck that attitude out of you anytime you want," he called after her.

Tears welled in Aria's eyes, but she didn't stop. She stormed across the studio quickly and right past Ben's assistant without even stopping to say hi. The moment she was in his office alone, she closed the door and burst into tears.

She didn't give a shit what Russell thought about her, though she hated how easily he still intimidated her. What really bothered her was that she was so afraid he was right. Not about dating Ben, because there's no way she'd ever leave him. She was falling for him—hell, she'd already fallen for him.

But about her career? Russell wasn't completely off base. If the press got wind of her romantic connections to Russell, Ben, *and* Travis, she'd be crucified.

Aria grabbed a tissue off the shelf of Ben's office and wiped her face, collapsing onto the couch with the bag of sandwiches. This was never how she'd meant for her career to go. She had given her heart away too carelessly, and now it was coming back to bite her.

It didn't matter that she'd earned her role on her talent. All that mattered was the perception, and honestly, she hadn't stacked the cards in her favor. *Fuck. If I was a man, this wouldn't be a problem.* She'd be lauded for her sexual prowess and playboy abilities if she had a damn penis.

Not that she had any sexual prowess, because she'd only ever slept with a small handful of men she'd been seriously involved with—or at least thought they'd been serious.

Aria wiped the last of the tears from her eyes, refusing to let even one more fall. She would not let Russell get the best of her. She would *not* let him psych her out. That was what he wanted, and he didn't get to win.

I've earned my career.

And I've earned the right to fall in love.

Aria set her jaw, taking a deep breath. Fuck anyone who told her differently.

CHAPTER TWENTY

"Good. You didn't run away." Ben walked into his office and caught sight of Aria on the couch. She was already halfway through her sandwich.

She glanced up at him, mouth full. "Sorry, I couldn't wait. I was starving."

Are her eyes red?

He took the seat next to her and grabbed his sandwich, beginning to unwrap it. "You okay?"

She shrugged but wouldn't look at him. "I'm fine. Unless you're getting back together with your wife. That would be decidedly *not* fine."

Ben chuckled. "Never going to happen. Marion just likes to tell stories. She's all about image, and likes people to see her in the most dramatic way possible. One of the many reasons she and I didn't work out."

Aria raised her sandwich to her mouth but, on second thought, put it down on the wrapper instead. "Tell me about that." She tucked her feet underneath her on the couch. "Why did you two get married in the first place?"

Ben swallowed the bite he was eating and cleared his throat. "Stupidity? If that can be an excuse. We just kind of went along with what the public expected from us because we didn't know what we actually wanted, or who we really were."

"And now?" Aria tilted her head to the side. "Do you know what you want?"

Honestly, he wasn't entirely sure, but he certainly knew what he didn't want—Marion. "I think I'm still figuring it out," he replied instead. "But for the first time, I'm not complacent. I'm not just going along to get to the end of the day or following expectations others have set for me. I'm excited about life again. I'm excited about you..." He reached out and rubbed his hand across her knee, putting his food down on the coffee table next to hers. "I'm *really* excited about you."

Crimson flooded her cheeks, the corners of her lips tilting into a smile. "Yeah? How...excited?" She slid a hand up his thigh to his groin, brushing against his cock which was already rock hard and uncomfortably pushing against his slacks.

"Aria..." he warned. "That door is not locked, and you've still got a shoot this afternoon."

Aria got to her feet, but never took her eyes off his. She sauntered to the door slowly and reached out. The click of the lock engaged echoed in the quiet office. "There. Locked." Her voice was so sultry it made his dick throb.

She walked over to his desk next and slid her hands down her thighs to the hem of her dress. Sliding her hands beneath, she wiggled slightly.

Her panties dropped to the floor and she picked them up with one finger, tossing them at him.

Ben was still sitting on the couch watching her, but he was already unbuckling his slacks because he feared he might rip a hole right through them if he didn't.

When she turned around, he thought he was done for, but he wasn't even remotely prepared for what was coming.

Aria grabbed the hem of her dress and flipped up the back, exposing her bare ass to him. The bunched-up fabric from her dress rested on her lower back and she leaned forward, placing both hands squarely on his desk. She turned her head to look at him over her shoulder.

She smirked. "Don't mess up my dress, and the photographer will never know."

He practically exploded off the couch, striding toward her with his pants undone and his shaft rock hard. "Jesus Christ, Aria. You're more than any guy could ask for."

"Good thing I don't want *any* guy," she teased, pushing back against him as he slid a hand between her legs. "Just you, Ben."

He growled, sliding two fingers against her core. She was already soaked, and he easily pushed inside her. "Say my name again."

She groaned, grinding back on his hand as he pumped in and out of her.

"Aria..." he warned. "Say. My. Name."

Her head fell forward, her breathing increasing. "Ben...Oh, God...Ben!"

He removed his hand, pressing himself against her entrance instead. Gripping her hips, he thrust inside her so hard they both fell forward into the desk.

She gasped, righting herself with her hands back on the desk's surface. Her core squeezed around him, and he was almost dizzy at how amazing she felt.

Reaching one hand around her body, he found her clit and became rubbing quick circles over it.

"Ben!" Aria jolted and began trembling, her climax overtaking her as she pulsed around his shaft. "Oh, God, I'm coming."

Pleasure barreled up his spine, making his eyes roll back as he approached his own climax. He was about to pull out, since their impromptu rendezvous hadn't come prepared with condoms, but she grabbed him and held him against her. "Come inside me, Ben. Please."

"Aria..." But it was too late, he slammed against her and dissolved into a million pieces as her own orgasm made her squeeze tight around his cock. "*Fuck.*" Ben groaned, his forehead against her back. "What did we just do?"

If he'd thought he wasn't ready for a single relationship, he most certainly wasn't ready for an entire family. Panic swelled inside him as his brain thought of every worst possible outcome, including both of their careers.

Aria laughed, light and sultry. "Relax. I got a birth control shot this morning—lasts three months."

Relief washed through him. "Oh. Okay, good. Not that I was worried."

"You were terrified," she teased, heading for the small private bathroom attached to his office to clean up.

"You have a shower in here?" Aria gasped a few minutes later, peeking her head out of the bathroom as he buttoned himself up.

"I'm big-time, baby," he teased, winking at her.

She raised one brow, sauntering back out of the bathroom and into his office. "Oh, I always knew you were big."

Ben laughed. "We should do lunch in my office more often."

Aria was already sitting and finishing the rest of her sandwich. "As long as it includes food, too — yes. A girl needs to eat."

He joined her on the couch, loving that she never shied away from food. She was thin, but not stick straight. She had natural curves and a soft, slightly rounded belly that he absolutely loved. Her confidence was so attractive, and another reason he loved her.

Love. That word again. It was getting harder *not* to say now.

Aria finished her sandwich and tossed the wrapper into the trashcan. "I've got to head back to set. I'm probably already late."

"Text me when you're done," he said, taking the last bite of his sandwich as well.

Aria pushed onto his lap, wrapping her arms around his neck. "Are you *telling* me, Ben Lawson? Or asking?"

"Not just telling...demanding." He swatted her ass. "Text me when you're done, because I've got plans for you tonight."

She giggled and covered his mouth with small, quick kisses. "Fine, but only because I want to. I rarely do what I'm told, Mr. Lawson."

"I am well aware."

She kissed him one more time. "You know, you're beginning to sound more and more like a boyfriend."

"I'd hope so," he replied, his tone more serious now. "You're mine, Aria."

She stared in his eyes for a minute longer, a smile on her lips. "Are you mine, Ben?" It was almost a whisper, and his heart warmed and burst with affection.

Ben slid his hands up her waist, holding her against him. "I've been yours since the first moment you smiled at me, baby."

When she smiled at that, he covered her lips with his. Soft, slow, sensual. He told her he loved her in that kiss, even if he wasn't quite ready to say it out loud.

She moaned against his mouth, then pushed on his chest. "I swear, if I don't leave now, we're going to end up locked in this office all afternoon."

"Can't have that," he teased.

Aria giggled, straightening her dress as she stood and then checking her reflection in the mirror. "It's not too obvious, is it?"

"Is what obvious?" Standing and walking back over to his desk.

"That I've just been fucked senseless, of course."

Ben burst out laughing, and shook his head. "You look practically virginal."

She scoffed. "Now I know you're lying."

Sitting behind his desk, Ben watched her leave. He tried to stifle his laughter when he heard her politely saying hello to Jackson as she passed his desk. Ben made a mental note to give his assistant a raise after what he'd most certainly heard.

The rest of the afternoon breezed by quickly. He was still riding high from "lunch" with Aria, and the satisfaction of having been able to tell off his ex-wife after she'd tried to manipulate Aria. She hadn't left quietly, but she'd gotten the message that he was involved with someone else now and wanted nothing to do with her.

"Hey, boss." A knock on his open door made him look up from the paperwork he was doing.

"Hey, Russ," Ben greeted the director. "What can I do for you?"

Russell Rains walked over to his desk and handed him a camera with the back screen lit up to a photo of Aria and Travis. "We had the photographer take a few fake candid photos of our lovebirds. Thinking it'd be a good idea to release them right after ticket pre-sales go live on Monday."

"Fake candid...so, you know they're not really dating?" Ben took the camera from him, surveying the image. Travis had his arms wrapped around Aria's waist and was kissing her right on the lips, both in their normal street clothes. Ben knew Travis wasn't a threat to him, but a small surge of jealousy still spread through him at the idea of anyone's mouth on Aria's.

"Well, yeah. They told me," Russell admitted, looking pretty sheepish for his usual cocky demeanor. He sat in the chair across from Ben. "But my lips are sealed. Scan through the photos and let me know if we have your approval to leak them."

Ben nodded, looking back down at the camera. Clicking through, he saw frame after frame of Travis and Aria laughing, cuddling, kissing, hugging. Swallowing, he turned off the screen. "These are fine."

"All of them? You looked at them all?" Russell asked.

He'd seen enough to know he couldn't see another man—even a gay man—all over his woman. "Yeah, they're great. And you've got their permission?"

Russell nodded, smiling wide. "Yep. They're all for it." He pulled a few papers out of a folder he'd been holding and laid them in front of Ben. "Sign these, boss, and we're good to go."

Ben scrawled his signature across the photo release forms, all pretty standard and mundane. "Okay. Done." Ben straightened the stack of papers and handed them back to Russell. "Let me know when they come out."

"Sure will." Russell stood and began heading for the office door, but then turned back to look at him. "Hey, Benji?"

Ben glanced back up. "Yeah?"

"You're doing a really great job here." A slow smile spread over Russell's face, excitement in his eyes that made Ben feel a little weird. *Was he hitting on him? Was it sarcasm?*

"Uh, thanks, Russell." Ben gave him a small wave. "Have a great evening."

"Night!" Russell left, practically skipping.

Ben frowned, but then pushed away the feeling of discomfort. Working with creative types often meant dealing with strange behavior — whether producers, directors, sound men, actors. They all shared an eclectic personality that served to make his life difficult. Luckily, he loved his job and he loved handling the talent.

That thought made him smile, because it was almost time for him to head home for the night and…handle the talent.

CHAPTER TWENTY-ONE

"Leave it," Steele told her. "I worked hard on that makeup."

"But the shoot is over," Aria reminded her friend while she finished changing into normal clothes in the small trailer.

"Right, but don't you have a hot date tonight?" Steele wiggled her brows at Aria, leaning against the makeup counter. "Ben will love it."

Aria's mouth fell open. *She knows?* "Ben? Uh...Ben...who's Ben?"

Steele rolled her eyes. "Girl, please. I love Travis—that man is one of the sweetest creatures I've ever known, but he's gay. Like...really, really gay."

Aria groaned. "Oh, God. Is it that obvious?"

"No. I'm just that good."

Aria chuckled and shook her head. "Please don't tell anyone. This just stays between us. Okay?"

"I would never out someone before they're ready," Steele assured her. "That's horrendous."

"I know you wouldn't. I just promised to keep his secret." Aria pulled a sweater on and fluffed out her hair. "My makeup does kind of look nice for a date night. Wait...how did you know I was dating Ben?"

"The way you stare at him like he's lunch, dinner, and dessert."

Aria laughed at the familiar metaphor. "I'm not as good an actress as I thought then."

"On stage, you're the best." Steele clasped her hands together dramatically. "Off stage? You're a girl in love."

"I am *not* in love," Aria quickly replied, rejecting the sentiment. A rush of nausea ran through her at the idea—wasn't it too soon? She was already worried she was going to ruin this whole thing.

Ben was barely a year out of a divorce, and his ex-wife was still showing up on the scene—literally. Not to mention they'd only spent a handful of days together, even if those days had been long and full of some of the most real conversations she'd ever had. Plus, the best sex of her entire freaking life.

Steele shook her head. "Well, like I said, I would never out someone. You're definitely in love, but if you're not ready to say it, then fine."

"I'm not ready to say it, because I am *not* in love. I'd be an absolute nut job if I was already in love so quickly. We've been dating like a month and a half, and most of that was spent apart."

"But the time you were together?" Steele asked.

Aria's lips twitched as her heart fluttered in her chest at the mere memory of it. "Magical."

"In love," Steele said in a singsong voice. "Aria's in love!"

"What!" Betty Reynolds walked into the trailer, her eyes wide. "Aria, what's the one with the tattoos saying?"

Steele rolled her eyes, snorting a little. Aria's mother and her best friend loved to jab at one another, but there was only love underneath their banter. "The one with the tattoos ain't saying a damn thing. Snitches get stitches."

Aria laughed at their exchange. "It's nothing, Mom. We were just joking around."

"I'm headed out, ladies. I'll be at your house by six on Monday morning, Aria. I'm doing your makeup for that audition, and I'm not taking no for an answer." Steele gave them both hugs before she left the trailer, closing the door behind her.

"Bye, Steele!" Aria called after her friend. "Hey, Mom, did you catch some of the shots? Any good?"

"Fantastic," her mother raved, both hands in the air. "I make beautiful children, you know. Are you coming over for dinner tonight? Friday night, I'm making the usual." She sang the words like a lure trying to reel her in.

Aria paused. Friday night was always pot roast night. Her favorite, but of course, her mother knew that. Her mouth watered in anticipation.

Memories surfaced of her date with Ben... and a different sort of hunger filled her. Electrical impulses flickered in her stomach then raced outward until her entire body was tingling at the thought of him. "I wish, but I've already made plans."

"Oh, really? With who? Because I know it's not Travis since I just caught him kissing the sound tech guy in his trailer."

"What?" A hint of annoyance prickled her, but it was tempered by a sense of pride. She loved that he was finding someone, but seriously, the more people who knew about their charade, the better their chances were of being discovered. "Well, good for him. At this rate, we'll be able to fake break up soon."

"And then you can tell me who it is you're really dating?"

"Mom..."

"Baby girl, you might be a big star soon, but you're never going to be too famous to have to listen to your mother." Betty opened the trailer door for them to head out, but a man was standing at the bottom of the steps, blocking them. "Oh. Hello, Mr. Lawson."

"Good evening, Mrs. Reynolds," Ben greeted her mother cordially, extending a hand and helping her down the rickety metal stairs that led to the trailer door. "How are you doing?"

"Just fine. I made a big dinner tonight and am trying to convince my daughter to come, but she's got other plans."

Aria mouthed *sorry* from behind her mother's back to Ben. She hadn't meant her mother to catch him here, or for him to get stuck in a long chat about pot roast.

Betty suddenly clapped her hands, gasping with excitement. "Oh, now here's an idea. Mr. Lawson, you should come to dinner with my family! Minus Aria, of course. Trim man like you, doesn't look like you've had a home cooked meal in a while."

Ben's mouth fell open and he stared awkwardly between her and her mother. "Um, I would love to, but I have made other plans, too. Thank you so much for the offer, though."

Suddenly, Betty swirled around and stared at Aria, then turned back to look at Ben. "Wait..."

"Mom..." Aria began to say, realizing her mother was putting the pieces together.

A grin spread over her mother's face, one brow lifted like she hadn't been fooled for a second. "Oh. I get it. Lovebirds want a Friday night to themselves." Betty hugged Ben tightly, catching him off guard. "I don't know why you're hiding him from *me*, Aria."

"I wasn't hiding." Aria sighed, shaking her head. Poor Ben looked like a deer in headlights with no clue what to say. "We're just keeping things private for now. Because of Travis."

"Well, I won't tell a soul. Mostly." Betty crossed her fingers over her heart. "But I am one happy mom. I hated the last guy you dated — Russ? God, he was the absolute worst. I still feel homicidal every time I see him here."

Ben's mouth fell open.

Shit! Aria couldn't breathe. She hadn't told him Ben about dating Russell. Not that it really mattered, because they hadn't talked to each other much about exes until the earlier drama with

Marion. Hearing about Russell from her mom, though? Not her best move.

"I'll see you Monday before the audition." Betty nonchalantly kissed Aria on the cheek, oblivious to the havoc she'd left behind. "See you soon for that dinner, I hope, Mr. Lawson."

"Yes, ma'am," he replied. "Have a great weekend."

The moment her mother was gone, Aria started walking toward the parking lot. "We should probably head out before we hit too much traffic."

"It's Los Angeles. There's always traffic." He kept pace with her, his body movements tense. They reached his car ten minutes later after a golf-cart ride and a short walk, glancing around to make sure no one saw them leaving together. He turned to her the moment the doors shut. "Okay. Explain."

"Do I have to?" Aria scrunched up her nose. "It's not a proud moment."

"Aria, you gave me so much grief about my ex showing up here. Meanwhile, your ex has been here every day. *We've been working with him?* You didn't think I should know that?"

"Honestly, no." She pulled her seatbelt on and buckled it. "It would have made things really awkward for you when you were working with him, and I didn't think that would be fair to you. He and I are long over, and really we were just a temporary blip on a very bad judgment radar."

He exhaled loudly, but said nothing as he latched his seatbelt then started the car. "Jesus. Russ? He's..."

"SO GROSS. I KNOW." Aria made a fake gagging noise. "I don't know what I was thinking. He was this big hot shot, all rock-and-roll and edge. I thought he was really interested in me, and I liked him. But, he was actually just sleeping with anything that moved."

"When was this?" He pulled the car out onto the main road.

"The first few weeks of rehearsal and filming. It was over fast."

Ben shook his head. "I cannot picture it. I can't picture you with that asshole. Period."

Aria threaded her fingers through the hair on the back of Ben's head as he drove, leaning closer to him. She caressed him gently, reflecting on her previous romance. "When I first came onto this project, I was lost. I had done a few movies—small parts—and a handful of commercials. I started seeing my entire career vanishing. Everything I'd worked so hard for since I was an early teenager...pointless. Russell made fame sound attainable. He helped me practice, and really worked with me on my craft. I wouldn't be the actress I am without him." She paused and frowned. "Which skeeves me out to say."

The car was silent for a moment. Finally, Ben rested his hand on her leg, squeezing gently. "Everyone has to have some redeeming qualities, I guess. If he helped you at the time, then great. But, babe?"

"Yeah?"

"I might punch him next time I see him."

Aria laughed, hoping he was joking, but also...kind of hoping he wasn't. "Hey, I could say the same thing about Marion, you know."

Ben tilted his head toward her. "You could, but I don't see you as the punching type."

"I wouldn't be so sure," she teased him and gave his hair a slight tug. "Travis and I were full-on plotting your murder earlier today when Marion implied you were getting back together."

Ben laughed, but there was a huskiness in his voice, and his eyes darkened the moment she'd tugged his hair. "I'm glad you have a friend who'd kill for you. Don't really love being the target, though."

"Don't worry. Your life was spared." She shot him a wide grin. "Hey, can I ask you an awkward question?"

Ben turned the car onto a small, darkened road. "Sure."

"Why didn't it work out with Marion? And what makes you think it would work out with...someone else...now?" She hated that she needed to know the answer to that, but it had been a thorn in her side for most of the day. Sure, he'd explained it a bit...but it hadn't been enough to ease her fears. "It's just...Marion and I seem similar. Like you have a type—actresses who are a little crazy. What if you and I—"

"You and Marion are nothing alike," Ben interrupted her, reaching for her hand and lacing their fingers together. "I may have a type—God help me—but only because movies are my world. It stands to reason that anyone I meet would be somehow involved in the film industry, whether an actress, or whatever."

"I know, but..."

"No buts. With Marion, everything was...methodic. If that makes sense. We were both playing a role we thought we needed, or that other people needed from us. There was no depth, no real bond." Ben's voice dipped slightly at the end — sadness?

Aria squeezed his hand tighter, wanting to comfort him.

"But with us, Aria," Ben continued, his voice stronger and more confident. "There's nothing easy about us. Nothing just for show. Everything is a jumble of emotions, and yet, it's wonderful because underneath it all is you...and me."

"We're bonded." Aria lifted his hand, still intertwined with hers, to her lips and kissed the back.

Ben put the car in park and leaned over to kiss her, soft and sweet. "We're completely fucking crazy, is what we are."

Aria laughed. He wasn't wrong.

Ben opened his car door. "Come on. I want to show you my house."

Realizing for the first time that they had arrived, Aria leaned forward to look out the windshield. *What. The. Actual. Fuckity. Fuck.* This wasn't a house. This was a fancy, giant prison. Unbuckling, she opened her car door and stepped out.

"Welcome to Casa Lawson." Ben gestured to the giant metal and concrete monstrosity.

While they walked up the strong steps, he told her about the architect that his ex-wife had hired to build it and how luxurious the house was, even though it wasn't really to his taste.

He wasn't wrong. Walking into the foyer, it was even more apparent how decadent the home was, and how much money it all must have cost. But...it...was...ugly...as fuck.

After a short tour around the main floor — kitchen, living room, dining room, each colder and darker than the last — Ben turned to her. "So, what do you think?"

Aria didn't say anything for a second, considering whether to lie and rave about the house he was clearly proud of, or tell him how much she despised every single thing about it. "Um...well...I think I understand why we always stay at my place."

Ben burst out laughing, a deep belly laugh that caused his head to tilt backward. "God, I love that you were honest. Truthfully, I hate this place. We spent so much time and money building it, but everything about it is Marion's taste, not mine."

"Why didn't she keep the home then?"

"She wanted to, but wouldn't be able to afford the taxes on it."

Aria headed for the staircase. "Maybe the bedroom isn't so bad?"

The bedroom was worse. So much fucking worse. Metal everywhere. It was so damn cold that her skin immediately broke out in tiny bumps.

"Ben, I hate your house."

He wrapped an arm across her shoulders. "Me, too. Want to head back to your place tonight instead?"

She shuddered. "God, yes."

Ben laughed and took her hand. "Let's go then. I'm officially calling my realtor in the morning and listing this place."

"Ben, no. You can't sell your house just because I don't like it."

"The hell I can't," he countered with a chuckle. "If my girlfriend hates it and I hate it, why on earth would I keep it?"

Aria's heart thumped a little harder in her chest. "I like when you call me that."

"Good. Get used to it, babe." He kissed her again as he wrapped his arms around her entire body, securing her against his chest. "I'm ready for this, Aria. I'm ready for a life of warmth and love. For the good and the bad. I'm ready to build a life around you, around us. I don't want anything else. I don't want anyone but you."

"Ben..." Aria's head was swimming, fear gripping her because damn it if she didn't feel exactly the same way. "We haven't known each other that long. This is crazy."

"Why is it crazy? We film movies all the time about people who meet and fall for each other...soul mates. Why is it crazy just because it's real this time?"

"I don't believe in soul mates, remember?" She hid her eyes from him, but the corners of her lips were tilted north.

"Liar." He tipped her chin up and met her gaze. Warmth flickered in his eyes. "Maybe you didn't before, but you believe in it now. You believe in *this*."

Her body trembled, and she swallowed hard, her chest rising and falling faster as he leaned toward her and placed his lips on hers. Circling his neck with her arms, she fell into his kiss. She fell into his promise, his security, his love.

He might not have said he loved her with his words, but everything about the way he held her, gazed at her, kissed her...he loved her. It was overwhelming and wonderful and terrifying and all too much, but she needed more.

She was beginning to come to terms with the fact that she was head-over-fucking-heels for Ben Lawson.

And maybe, just maybe, she *was* starting to believe in soul mates.

CHAPTER TWENTY-TWO

Aria woke with a jolt, looking around her dark bedroom. As her senses slowly began to adjust, she looked for the source of whatever had disturbed her. Her cell phone vibrated against the surface of her nightstand, its screen casting a square light onto the ceiling above.

Yawning, she grabbed for it, glancing over at the man in bed next to her, her heart filling with warmth at the sight of Ben's sleeping form. Yesterday had been a dream, as it always was between them. They'd spent their entire Saturday either in bed, on the beach, or in the shower. There was a delicious, dull ache between her legs from how many times they'd been together, but that did nothing to temper how much she still wanted him.

Weekends with Ben were quickly becoming her favorite pastime.

She ran a hand down his naked back as he slept sprawled on his stomach, his head turned in her direction. She leaned over and kissed his cheek and he stirred, but didn't wake. Long, dark lashes rested peacefully on his face—not a care in the world in his expression.

Just pure happiness.

Aria put a hand to her chest, feeling the thump behind her ribs. Sometimes she needed to remind herself that this was really happening—she was really falling in love with a wonderful man who she could trust and give her whole self to.

It was new territory for her. She'd always been so guarded in relationships, but with Ben...she didn't feel the need to be.

She felt safe.

She felt loved.

She was *in* love.

Pulling away from her self-indulgent thoughts, Aria finally focused on her phone. Furrowing her brow, she realized she had dozens of missed texts, calls, and emails.

"What the hell?" she whispered to herself, sitting up. She pulled the sheet with her, covering her naked body with the thin linen as she propped her elbows on her knees and scrolled through all her missed notifications.

Aria, are you awake? WAKE UP NOW.

Don't look at the news. We need to talk. 911.

Is that you on E! News? Did you allow that?

OMG, ARIA! WHAT THE HELL?

What did you do?!?! This is career suicide!

Her heart began to race, panic swarming her every cell as she quickly clicked out on a website link that Steele had sent her, the first text she'd received.

A photo popped up. Then another. And another, and another, and Aria knew exactly what she was looking at.

Herself.

Nude.

Aria could barely breathe, trembling as she searched social media and entertainment news sites from her phone. She prayed that it was an anomaly—only one site had them and no one else. This wasn't wide spread. She could fix this.

The photos were everywhere.

Every entertainment site was carrying the story, the photos. She was trending on social media, and everyone had an opinion to share. None of them kind.

Her breasts, her body, her love life on full display for the world to see. It would have been bad enough if they'd just been images of her posing nude, but these were pornographic. These were her in her most intimate moments with a man she'd...

Did he do this? Why? A sob stuck in her throat. She looked at the man still sleeping beside her, fear gripping her heart.

This couldn't be happening.

If Ben found out about these photos, he'd never forgive her. He'd never see her the same way again—how could he? She was disgusted with herself right now almost as much as all the trolling comments from people online calling her a slut and a whore.

Articles were debating who was in the photos with her, but she knew. Crawling out of her bed as quietly as she could so as not to disturb Ben, she quickly got dressed and closed herself off in the bathroom, dialing her mother.

"Mom?" Her voice shook, her eyes already welling with tears. "Mom, I'm so sorry. I didn't know...I didn't mean to..."

She didn't even know what she was apologizing for, but embarrassment flooded her at the thought of her parents seeing those photographs. Her sisters, oh god. She'd always wanted to be a role model to her sisters—that was ruined now.

"Don't be sorry, baby," Betty said over the line, her tone the exact calmness Aria needed right now. "Come to my house right away. I'm sending a car and security to get you here. They'll be there in ten minutes. We'll fix this, okay?"

Panic clutched at her. "How? It's everywhere, Mom. I'm..."

"Aria, have I ever failed you before? No. I'm your manager, yes, but I'm your mom first. And I'm going to help you fix this, okay? Do you trust me?"

"Of course I do."

"Then trust that it'll be okay. And, baby girl?" Her mother paused for a moment, then sniffed. "I'm so sorry this is happening to you. I love you. Your daddy loves you. Nothing has changed. Understand? We love you no matter what."

Aria burst into tears, her hand over her mouth to muffle the sounds. Relief flooded her at their unconditional support and love. "Thank you, Mom."

"I'll see you soon, sweetheart." The line went silent.

Aria looked at herself in the bathroom mirror and washed her face. The sun wasn't even up yet, so there was no way she was going to wake up Ben. She didn't want him knowing about any of this. For a minute, she considered dropping his phone in a glass of water.

Running her hands through her hair, she groaned. There was no point. He'd find out from someone. At least she could hold it off as long as possible, and not be here to see the look of disgust and disappointment on his face when he did find out.

Sneaking back into the bedroom, Aria turned off Ben's phone and replaced it on the nightstand. She quickly grabbed a small bag of clothes, changing into casual sweats and an oversized sweatshirt.

Her phone lit up with a text from the driver her mother had sent. Tossing her wallet and phone into her bag, she slung it over her shoulder and headed for the front door. When she swung it open, there was a security guard standing there with a cup of coffee and a small bag that smelled like warm muffins.

"Good morning, Miss Reynolds. I'm here to take you to your mother's house." He handed her the coffee. "She insisted I bring you breakfast."

"Of course she did." Aria chuckled, enjoying the small reprieve of emotions. She locked her apartment door and then followed him down to the lobby of her building.

"We're going out the back." He motioned for a back door she rarely took. "Too many reporters out front."

"Seriously? They're already here?" Aria felt her stomach turning. "This is a disaster."

"Duck your head and grab the back of my shirt. Don't stop moving until you're in the back seat. Got it?" he instructed her right before opening the back door. "There's bound to be a few back here, too."

The moment he swung the door open, lights flashed in her face and questions were hurled at her. She clutched the guard's shirt—grateful for the advice, since she'd be blind otherwise—and in seconds, she was shoved into the back of a car. The entire thing lasted less than two seconds, and yet, it was the most stressful two seconds of her entire life.

She'd dealt with the occasional paparazzi before, but never so many at once. There'd never been such an interest in her before, and she was both devastated and furious that nude photos were the thing that had pushed her into the spotlight.

"Windows are tinted, ma'am," the driver told her after he'd climbed into the front seat, and passed the bag of muffins back to her. "So, you're safe."

"Thank you." She leaned against the leather seat back and took a sip of the warm coffee and a bite of the muffin. The car was pushing through throngs of reporters slowly.

Freaking insane.

"I can't even believe this," she whispered to herself, watching reporters trying to film the car and stop her for a question. She couldn't hear them very well—mostly muffled thanks to the car's interior, but she caught the occasional word from reading lips and none of it was kind.

They were ravenous, wanting to rip her apart for the sake of ratings and website clicks. Not a single empathetic face in front of her—they only wanted to feast on her remains to pad their bank accounts.

Her career was over before it had even begun.

CHAPTER TWENTY-THREE

Ben stretched an arm out across the bed to pull Aria close to him. An insatiable need drove him when it came to her, and he was quite certain now that it would never be quenched. He needed her, wanted her, had to have her as often as he possibly could.

Instead of finding her warm, slumbering body next to him, his hand fell against the cold sheets. Blinking his eyes open, he yawned and looked around the room.

Sitting up, he realized he was alone. *Strange.*

Ben turned and placed his feet on the floor, shivering slightly at the cool wood beneath his feet as he located his clothes. He tugged on a pair of pants, opting for no shirt yet, and headed out to the living room to find Aria.

But a quick walk around the small apartment revealed she wasn't there.

A scowl tugged at his brow, unease settling in his gut. *Maybe she was on a breakfast run?* Patting his pockets, he couldn't find his cell phone. The clock on the wall in her kitchen revealed it was almost noon.

Crap. He hadn't meant to sleep in that late.

Returning to the bedroom, he found his phone on her nightstand. His initial ease turned to full-blown frustration when he realized his phone was off. *Did I forget to charge it overnight?* He felt around the back of the nightstand for the phone charger plugged into the wall, but there was nothing there. Peering behind it, he saw the charger on the ground.

Why would I pull it out of the wall? The answer was that he wouldn't. Frustration slowly dissipated into fear, an unfamiliar feeling swarming his gut as he plugged his phone in and sat on the edge of the bed, waiting for it to turn back on.

The screen lit up several excruciatingly long minutes later. "Finally," he muttered, gritting his teeth. He noted a few missed calls and texts, but bypassed them when he saw none of them were from Aria. Instead, he dialed her number.

The phone rang three times, then went to voicemail. "You've reached Aria Rose. Please leave a message after the—"

Ben hung up before it clicked to voicemail. Opening his texts, he sent her a quick message asking where she was. He waited a minute to see if she read it, but the text wouldn't even confirm it had been delivered.

Feeling more and more anxious, Ben began flipping through his other missed messages. He was a little surprised he had so many missed messages for a Sunday morning, but he and Aria had spent most of the day in bed yesterday ignoring the outside world, so it wasn't too unusual.

Until he realized why.

Ben's body went stiff, every muscle locking into place as he clutched the phone tighter in his hand. His other fist knotted in the bed sheet next time, nearly tearing the fabric in two. "WHAT THE FUCK?"

Rage misted his vision red for several seconds before he could gather enough control to read through everything in front of him. This could *not* be happening.

Nude photos of Aria had gone viral overnight.

Not just nude, actually. These were candid shots of her having sex with...*I'll kill him! That fucking bastard!* The internet was abuzz trying to figure out who the mystery man was, but Ben recognized the long, curly, black hair immediately. He'd worked with him for weeks.

Russell.

A fury stronger than he'd ever felt before slammed through Ben's body, and he jumped up from the bed, gathering the rest of his clothes and roughly pulling them on. He slammed the bedroom door into the wall with a loud bang as he stormed into the living room and grabbed his keys, heading for the front door.

Aria had tried to convince him her relationship with Russell was in the past—hell, she even said he'd helped her. Ben had given her the benefit of the doubt, but he had never liked Russell. And now? He fucking hated him.

The fact that that bastard could do this to Aria — let alone any woman — made Ben sick.

Wait until I get my hands on him. Anger clouded Ben's vision as he charged down the stairs and out the front door of Aria's apartment complex.

"Is that Ben Lawson?" someone called out the moment he stepped onto the sidewalk. "Ben Lawson? Head of Shepherd Films?"

Flashes started going off in his face, and Ben stepped back, shocked. *What the hell?*

"MR. LAWSON, WHAT ARE YOU DOING COMING OUT OF ARIA ROSE'S HOME? ARE YOU SLEEPING WITH HER, TOO?"

Fuck! Ben steeled himself and walked briskly the rest of the way to his car, dodging the few photographers and paparazzi who seemed to have set up camp outside her building.

"Just business," he said loudly, hoping they'd buy it. Their expressions were dubious.

Climbing into his car, he quickly sped off and away from the cameras, hoping he hadn't made everything worse. Guilt swallowed him whole as he pointed his car toward the highway. He should have considered that photographers would be staking out her apartment now, but he'd been so livid, it hadn't even crossed his mind.

Now he might have romantically linked her to the executive in charge of her movie, not to mention she was still publicly involved in that fake relationship with Travis. And now these photos with Russell.

The fall out is going to be astronomical. Especially if they didn't buy his business story and painted her as someone who sleeps her way into roles—which of course was the furthest thing from the truth. Aria had earned everything she had because of her talent and hard work.

Ben cringed, feeling sick at the thought of what Aria must be experiencing right now. He needed to talk to her.

Grabbing his phone, he dialed her again. Still no answer. This time, he stayed on the line until the voicemail clicked on. "Aria, I just heard the news. I am so, so sorry. Please call me. I can fix this. I'll freaking kill him! Call me, Aria."

He hung up and quickly dialed Arthur next.

"Bloody hell, Ben. We're in deep today," Arthur said the moment the line clicked through.

"Tell me about it." Ben groaned. "I need Russell Rain's address. Now. Text it to me."

"Why? Oh, wanker. He's the bloke in the photos with her?"

"Just text me the address, Arthur. And talk to whoever you need to talk to about getting those photos off the internet. We'll pay any price."

"On it, boss." The line disconnected, and a second later, a beeping sound told him Arthur had sent the address.

Coordinating it into his car's GPS, Ben broke every speed limit on his way. It was no secret Russell had a sleazy side, but this was beyond anything Ben could have imagined. *It doesn't make any goddamn sense!*

Scarlet's Letters was Russell's film as much as it was the studio's, and this would tank everything he'd worked so hard for as well. This was his livelihood he was messing with—for what? A vendetta? A sick joke? A sadistic ploy?

Fucking idiot! Ben slammed his hand against the steering wheel.

He needed Shepherd Films turned around in the first year, and this film was supposed to be the key. He couldn't believe his own director had destroyed that—and possibly Ben's entire career along with it.

As furious as he was at Russell, he was also furious at himself. He'd promised to protect Aria, and instead, he'd let someone completely take advantage of her in the worst possible way. He'd slept half the day away while she was out there alone trying to remedy her ravaged reputation.

He'd failed to protect her. After all his promises.

This was his fault.

CHAPTER TWENTY-FOUR

Ben's car raced up the long driveway to Russell's home overlooking the ocean in Orange County. The decadence that stretched out in front of him brought Ben's already heated blood to a fast boil. It was one of the most beautiful houses he'd ever seen—and fucking Russell didn't deserve an inch of it.

Hell, he deserved jail.

When Ben was done with him, he'd turn him over to the cops, and then he'd find Aria and do whatever he could to help her get through this. Driving the front tires of his car directly onto one of Russell's rose bushes, Ben honked his horn several times before he threw the car into park and climbed out.

Ben clenched his fists as he stalked up the long walkway to the front door, the warm breeze from the ocean fueling his fury. The perfectly landscaped flower beds he stalked passed sawed at his nerves, and he almost turned around to get back in his car and drive over every inch of his shrubbery rather than only the roses he'd murdered moments ago with the front end of his car.

Destroy his flowers? Have I lost my fucking mind? He didn't want flowers.

Ben wanted blood.

His fists balled as he took the stairs up to the porch two at a time, ready to break it down if he had to.

The front door to the giant Spanish-style home swung open and a half naked Russell walked out wearing only a pair of linen pants and bohemian jewelry around his neck and wrists. "What the fuck? Who's honking?" He looked over at Ben's car, then at Ben, and a knowing leer crept over his face. "Well, hi there, Benji."

Ben's arm coiled his back, then launched himself forward. His fist slammed directly into Russell's face with a loud, satisfying *crack*.

"AAAH! Motherfucker!!" Russell stumbled, clutching his nose. Blood was already gushing over his mouth and jaw. "You broke my fucking nose, you crazy bastard."

"WHY WOULD YOU RELEASE THOSE PHOTOS, RUSSELL?" Ben shouted, not stepping away, but rather forcing Russell to keep moving backward until Ben had him cornered against the tan stucco wall by his front door. "WHY?"

Russell spit blood out on the white marble floor of his front stoop. "Shit, Benji. You could have just fucking asked me that without the fanfare. I'm a pacifist, you know."

What the fuck is he talking about? Ben's mind was swimming with rage, and Russell seemed completely calm. In pain, definitely, but any other emotional reaction was nonexistent. *Fucking psychopath.* "Do you seriously not give a shit about Aria? About what you just did to her career? You hate her that fucking much?"

Russell frowned, seeming confused. "Are you kidding? I love Aria. I've been in love with her for over a year, and now the whole world knows it."

Ben's mouth fell open, trying to process the information.

"She would have forgiven me and come around," Russell continued, his voice gurgling as he was still holding his bleeding face. "You're the one who fucked that up for me. I see the way she looks at you. Now the whole fucking world can see how she looked at me...*first.*"

Ben punched him again. Square in the jaw this time.

"Motherfucker! Stop that shit!" Russell tumbled back into the wall. "Seriously! I'm going to punch you back."

"DO IT." Ben didn't stand down. "I dare you, you piece of shit."

"Listen, Benji. You gotta stop taking everything so personal. This is just business." Russell was holding his chin in his hand now, massaging it gently. "Fuck, that last one really hurt."

"*Just business?* This was your film, Russell. Just as much as it was mine or the studio's, or Aria's. You took all of us down with this leak."

"Even bad press is good press, Benji."

Ben was certain in that moment that Russell might be the stupidest, most evil person he'd ever fucking met.

"I'm calling the police. You're going to jail for this, Russell. I know there's no way Aria approved those photos." Ben began walking toward his car, leaving a bleeding Russell on his front stoop.

"She didn't approve them," Russell called after him. "You did."

Ben whirled around and charged back toward the director. "What did you just say?"

Russell's sly grin showed a row of crimson-stained teeth from the blood dripping into his mouth. "It was your idea to leak the photos to the media." His voice got louder, and Ben took a small step back, unsure what Russell was saying, or why he'd raised his volume. "You were right, Benji. The photos did exactly what you thought they would. I'm glad you approved them before they went out. Selling Aria's tits to the tabloids was the best idea you've ever had."

Ben's mind immediately began clicking through the other afternoon in his office when he'd approved photos of Travis and Aria to be leaked to the press. *Holy fuck. I didn't look at all the photos.*

A soft gasp behind him pulled Ben from his thoughts. He turned to see Aria standing in the middle of the driveway, her hand on her throat. Her blue-gray eyes were wild, devastated, confused.

"Oh. Hi, sweet pea," Russell greeted her, still trying to wipe the blood from his face.

She didn't look at him, her focus solely on Ben. "Is it true?"

Ben wanted to rush to her, pull her into his arms and assure her that he'd never do anything like that to her. He'd promised to protect her, and he'd never break that. She could trust him.

Except he had done it.

"Ben? Tell me it isn't true. Tell me he's lying," she repeated, desperation in her strained voice. "Please, Ben."

Swallowing hard, he stared at her, unable to speak. He shook his head, searching his brain for anything...damn it, *anything*. "I...I didn't mean..."

A sob ripped from her throat and tears began to slide down her pale cheeks. "Oh, my God. How could you?"

"Baby, don't worry," Russell interjected. "Everyone loves a scandal. Ticket sales are going to be through the roof."

Ben shoved Russell behind him, and rushed toward her. "Aria, I never meant—"

"Don't touch me!" She jumped back, suddenly shouting. Turning on her heel, she began walking to her car which he now saw was parked behind his.

"Aria!" he shouted after her, but didn't follow her.

"Don't come near me ever again—either of you!" Then she was in her car, speeding down the driveway and out of sight.

Ben stood there, watching her go, taking his heart with her. A lump filled his throat as he realized she would never forgive him, and he'd never forgive himself. There was no coming back from what he'd done, even if it was a mistake.

They were over.

The woman he loved, the future he'd pictured, the dream he'd had for them...it was all gone.

Because of him.

"Awkwaaaard," Russell said in a singsong tone behind him. "Women, am I right?"

A woman stepped into the open doorway, shaking her head. "Jeez, even *I* thought that was dramatic."

"Marion?" Ben's mouth fell open as he realized his ex-wife had just witnessed the entire scenario. Somehow, the worst days of his life always seemed to involve her. "You're with Russell now?"

She shrugged, a total lack of empathy on her face. "He's putting me in his next movie."

Fucking typical.

"See, Benji? With such similar taste in pussy, we should be friends." Russell draped an arm across Marion's shoulder.

Ben punched him again, knocking him flat on his back this time.

Marion jumped to the side, catching herself from being dragged to the ground with Russell. "Jesus, Ben! Control yourself!"

"You two deserve each other," Ben told her, seething with disgust. He turned to Russell and pointed a finger at him. "I'm so far from fucking done with you, you piece of shit. You're fired."

Russell grunted, coughing as he tried to push himself back up. His face spread into a bloody, sinister smile. "You can't fire me. The movie's over."

Partially true, but damn it if Ben wouldn't find any loophole possible to get this bastard off his movie. "You're fucking done in Hollywood. I won't rest until you're either blacklisted from every studio out there, or in fucking jail."

Ben headed back to his car, desperately trying to think of his next move. He wanted to find Aria, and beg her forgiveness. He wanted to explain everything.

He wanted this not to be the end, and yet, the deep ache in his heart told him it was.

And he'd never forgive himself for it.

CHAPTER TWENTY-FIVE

"Aria, honey?" Her mother stuck her head through the doorway to Aria's childhood bedroom. "Are you awake yet? Steele is here."

Aria had been awake for hours. Actually, she'd never slept. She'd laid in bed all night trying to process how her life had fallen apart so easily in the last twenty-four hours. Her apartment was still surrounded by paparazzi, so she'd had no choice but to seek refuge at her parent's house which, thankfully, was in a gated community. In her childhood bed. Like a sulking teenager again.

It was pathetic. She was pathetic.

Every major entertainment news site had run with the story accompanied by her photographs by the time she'd woken up on Sunday, and she had no doubt it would still be a hot topic today. People picked apart her appearance, her personality, her promiscuity, her sexuality, and her career. They all had an opinion about her, like she was a commodity they could trade rumors for dollars.

Her mother and sisters had tried to help her all day yesterday with damage control. Releasing a statement that the photos were a hack and without her permission. Police report filed and statement given. She'd even gone to Russell's house to punch him, but Ben had beat her to it. And then, of course, she'd found out about Ben's involvement. That the man she loved had released her nude photos to the public...for what? Ticket sales? Box office ratings?

Talk about a gut punch.

She'd thought she knew Ben. She'd never felt so strongly about a man before—that intensity, that passion, that confidence that he...fit. But, the reality was she barely knew him. Truthfully, they'd just spent a quick frenzy of long, wonderful days wrapped around each other in bed with even longer periods of absence between.

Once again, she'd trusted the wrong man. It was starting to become a pattern about herself she didn't like. This wasn't who she thought she'd be. This wasn't who she'd ever wanted to be. Her mother was one of the strongest women she knew, and she'd raised all her daughters to be independent self-starters.

She hadn't raised her to lose everything because of a man. Twice.

"Aria?" Steele's voice finally got her to turn around. "Are you doing okay?"

Aria sat up on the bed, rubbing her eyes. "No. Not even a little."

"Do you want me to cancel the audition today?" Her mother asked from the doorway, looking as tired as Aria felt. She wondered if her mother had been awake all night too, and guessed she probably had.

"There's no way they're going to hire me." Aria sighed, shaking her head. "They won't want someone with such bad press."

"Are you kidding?" Steele scoffed. "You're the best. They're going to want you because of your talent. Everyone has...um, skeletons in their closet. This is Hollywood. You haven't made it until you've got a sex tape."

Aria chuckled a little at that. "Please, God, let there not be a tape."

"If there is, I'll personally strangle his skinny little neck," Steele assured her, wrapping an arm around her shoulders.

"I think Steele's right. You should do the audition," her mother added. "And I'm not saying this as your manager. I'm saying this as your mother. This man...he took something from you. If we lie down and let him, he'll take everything. Go to the audition. Take your power back, baby girl. Show the world this won't break you."

Aria stared at her mother, feeling a small surge of confidence from the way she spoke.

Steele bobbed her head, waving her arms in the air emphatically. "Preach, Mama Reynolds. Fucking preach!"

Her mother laughed. "I'm going to head downstairs and set up the dining room table for you to use as a makeup station, Steele."

"Thanks," Steele replied, then turned to Aria. "You hop in the shower, okay? Then meet me downstairs? Your mother made these delicious egg bite things, and I swear to God if you don't hurry, I'm going to eat them all."

Aria smiled, nodding. "I'll be down in a few."

Alone, Aria headed for the shower, shedding her clothes along the way and leaving them wherever they fell. The warm water beat down on her head and back, and she took a moment just to feel it. Just to embrace the soothing massage of its pressure on her skin.

Tears slid down her cheeks, and she let them come. She let them mix with the shower water and fall to the tile floor, disappearing down the drain and taking her pain with it.

When she stepped from the shower and wrapped a towel around her head, she paused in front of the full-length mirror.

Nude.

Until yesterday, she'd never felt much self-consciousness about her naked body. As a teenager, she'd gone through her phases, but once she'd reached adulthood, she'd embraced who she was.

She'd had to. Being an actress was cutthroat. Every audition, every fitting — it could destroy her self-esteem if she let it. And until yesterday…she hadn't let it. There were so many comments online following the leak of her nude photos, each more brutal than the next.

She must wear padded bras. Tiny tit bitch.
Boob job! Stat!

Aria brushed her hands over her breasts, cupping them and feeling their weight. They weren't tiny, but they weren't huge either. This wasn't the first time someone had poked fun of them—mainly Russell came to mind. He'd loved to remind her of everything she...lacked.

Aren't actresses supposed to have personal trainers? Someone teach this cunt how to do some crunches.

She'd grown to love the swell of her small breasts, and the roundness of her belly that was just a few pounds shy of flat. Her hands slid across her belly, smooth and dewy from her shower.

I'd bite the fuck out of that giant ass! I bet she can make those hips move!

Fat ass. Lay off the donuts, slut.

Bet that cunt loves getting it in the ass. I'd throw her a pity fuck if she begs me.

Aria's hands passed over her hips, and then her bottom. She loved her wide hips and voluptuous backside. They were natural, healthy, and normal. She was a far cry from overweight, and she didn't want those comments to get to her, but...

No. She wasn't going to let internet trolls ruin the self-esteem she'd spent a lifetime building. She wasn't going to let the crass things men said about her touch her.

But that was the easy part.

As a woman, she'd been raised her whole life to ward off men's advances and build her shield against predators. More than half the comments she'd read attacking her...they were from women.

And she didn't have shields for the betrayal of her own gender yet. She'd never needed them before.

Friendships with women had always come easy for her, and she was a big believer in the power of sisterhood since she came from a tight-knit family of women. But, if she could believe the online commentary, it felt as if her entire gender had turned on her just as much—if not more.

Repeating her mother's words in her head, Aria decided she wasn't going to let those photos— or Russell, or the press, or Ben, or anyone in those awful online comments—tell her who she was or judge her body. She refused to be broken by their collective betrayal.

She knew who she was.

She was going to go into that audition just like she would have before any of this happened. She was going to ace it and get the role. She was going to prove that she was above one damn scandal. She was going to prove that she was the best for the part—that simple.

So that's how she got the part. She sucked his dick!

No talent hack. Has to fuck her way into a movie. Pathetic!

Stick to porn. You suck at acting.

This is why no one takes us women seriously. Stop using your body to get what you want and grow some brain cells. Or better yet—talent!

Aria swallowed, trying to push the nerves in her stomach away. She could do this, right? She could rise above those words. She...wasn't so sure.

Damn it.

She wished it was as easy as her mother made it sound. That she could just hold her head up high and forget the things they'd called her, the assumptions they'd made, the pictures he'd spread.

It simply wasn't that easy.

"Aria, you coming?" Steele called from somewhere downstairs.

Aria pulled on a silk robe and let her hair out of the towel. "Coming."

"Hey, honey bunny," her father greeted her as she reached the bottom of the stairs. He was propped up in a recliner in front of the television in the living room, mostly immobile because of multiple sclerosis these days. Never dampened his spirits, though. "How are you feeling?"

"Tired." She gave him a kiss on the cheek.

He chuckled. "Well, it's like five in the morning."

"I know. Gotta prep for this audition, but what are *you* doing up?" She refilled his glass of water for him and brought it back to the small stand next to his chair.

"Oh, you know your mother. Neither of us could sleep a wink last night thinking about..."

Aria sat on the edge of the coffee table, facing her father. "Dad, I'm so sorry. I'm...God, I'm horrified at what you must think of me."

Her father's face scrunched up and he sighed. "Aria, I haven't seen the photos or anything. God knows I wouldn't want to, and I made your mother promise to hide any of that from me."

"Good!" Aria was relieved to at least know that much.

"But...knowing they are out there? None of that makes me think any less of you, Aria. There were two people in that room—the blame for what occurred between you two is not yours to carry alone."

She swallowed, sniffing lightly. "I know, but you should see the things they're saying, Daddy. All of it is...she's a slut, he's a playboy."

"Fuck that shit." Her dad tossed his arm up in the air with a dramatic flair. "Fuck all of them. Nothing wrong with what you did. Now, what *he* did? First, taking the photos and then releasing them? Downright criminal, and I hope he rots in prison, because I swear to God if he doesn't I'll kill him my damn self."

Aria laughed and moved to give her father a hug. "Thank you, Daddy."

He hugged her back, gently ruffling her hair with his hand. "I love you, baby girl. No matter what. Nothing can ever change that."

"Aria, you ready?" Steele popped her head into the living room. "Oh, shit. Am I ruining a moment? Go back to your moment."

Aria and her father both laughed.

"Go get ready for that audition," he told her. "You're going to kill it."

"Thanks, Daddy." Aria followed Steele into the dining room which was entirely covered in hair and makeup accessories, along with a rack of clothes against the wall. "Holy crap, Steele."

"I know. I brought everything. Made Xavier carry it all in here for me, too." She ran her hands across the row of clothes. "He's out getting us all some coffee and donuts."

"No donuts for me." Aria quickly shook her hands in front of her body, then patted her stomach. "I really should drop a few pounds."

Steele huffed and took a step back. "Aria, I swear on every tattoo on my goddamn body that if you let those internet troll comments get in your head, I will slap you silly."

Warmth rushed to Aria's face as she took a seat at the table facing her friend. "Okay, okay. Maybe half a donut."

"You're going to eat an entire goddamn donut with extra icing and you're going to fucking like it," Steele threatened, pointing a giant makeup brush at her. "Now, close your eyes because I'm about to prime the fuck out of those glorious cheekbones."

Aria laughed, already feeling a million times better than she'd felt all day yesterday. Good friends and family...she was beginning to realize that that was all that really mattered in this world.

Ben. Russell. Every man who'd hurt her. Every woman who'd looked down on her. She didn't need them. She didn't want them, and damn it, she'd be just fine without them.

At least, that was what she was going to tell herself today.

Today, she was focusing on the audition, and nothing else. This wouldn't be the moment her career ended. Russell wouldn't be the one who'd take it all from her.

She'd earned every moment of her career, and if she was going down, she was going down fighting.

CHAPTER TWENTY-SIX

"That's unacceptable, Arthur!" Ben paced back and forth in his office early Monday morning, his hands rubbing across the top of his head. "This is on us. *It's on me.* I have to fix this."

"Don't you think I know that?" Arthur's gruff English accent was even thicker with the stress they were under. "The liability on the company is astronomical. This could bankrupt us if she sues."

Ben stopped in his tracks and turned to face his right-hand man. "*If* she sues us? She *should* sue us. We deserve it—I deserve it."

"Damn it, Lawson. Enough with the self-flagellation. I get it. You're the big boss and this is on your shoulders, but for Christ's sake, son. She's just an actress, and they are just some photos. Not that unusual in the grand scheme of things."

Ben gripped the edge of the desk, trying to calm himself, but his words came out stilted and furious. "She. Is. Not. Just. A. Fucking. Actress!"

NUDES: A HOLLYWOOD ROMANCE

Arthur narrowed his eyes for a moment, then pointed at him. "Oh, bloody hell. So, you weren't just shagging her? You went and caught feelings? We're up to our fuckin' eyeballs in liability right now!"

Ben didn't reply, sagging into his desk chair instead. He picked a pen up from the desk, tapping it against his knee as he tried to think of a solution.

They'd managed to recall a lot of the photos yesterday and last night, removing them from the majority of websites and convincing the rest to censor the photos with black bars. It had cost thousands upon thousands of dollars, and every man on deck, but they'd at least managed that much. Today was the start of the week though, and certainly the damage control was just beginning since the originals would always be out there, and God knows how many downloads or screenshots.

Ben groaned, overwhelmed at the scope of the disaster they were facing. He rubbed his hands over his face for the hundredth time, trying to collect his thoughts.

Aria hadn't returned his phone calls since he'd last seen her at Russell's house yesterday. And now her phone number was disconnected today. Not that he was surprised. The number of calls she'd probably gotten from the press could have made her have to switch numbers.

Or she'd just blocked him. Either way, he was fucking miserable.

He'd tried to visit her apartment again, but it was still surrounded by reporters, and her car was nowhere in sight. Ben guessed she was staying with her family, but he didn't know where they lived and strongly doubted showing up on their porch would go over well right now.

"I think we should push for charges," Ben finally suggested.

"Against Rains?"

Ben nodded. "At the very least, he needs to be let go from the project. Publicly."

Arthur frowned, unconvinced. "Filming is already wrapped. It would be pointless. It's mainly..."

"Symbolic. Exactly." Ben stood from his desk again, unable to get comfortable. "That's the point. That this behavior isn't tolerated. It's not the type of message that resonates with *Scarlet's Letters*, and it's not the type of person we want involved with our studio."

"We'd have to pay him off. He's got us hooked in his contract now that he's delivered his end." Arthur mused, but seemed to be warming to the idea as Ben continued to pace back and forth. "But...it could work."

"If we have to, we will. Money isn't worth our morals." Ben stopped at his window, staring out onto the lot stretching out below. "But have the lawyers scour his contract anyway. A morality clause. A loophole. Anything. If there's a way out— find it."

"On it," Arthur said, already pulling his phone out of his pocket and dialing as he stood and headed for the office door. "In the meantime, Lawson, keep your 'feelings' for Miss Rose private. I know some people mentioned you in the press, but, so far, it just looks like they are throwing out a large net to see what they'll catch. If you don't give them the bait, they won't find the story."

Ben nodded, watching Arthur go.

There wasn't any story left to find anyway. He and Aria were over. She'd made that very clear on the front steps of Russell's home — and he understood.

If there was ever a way to redeem his actions, he would find it, but so far, he was coming up empty. He couldn't imagine a world in which Aria — or any woman — could what he'd done, or what he'd let happen.

He wanted to explain, wanted to tell her he hadn't known what he was doing, and that it was a horrible accident. But that really didn't matter. It didn't make anything better. It didn't change what he'd done, and it didn't change the damage he'd caused her. His carelessness had not only been a failing as a studio head, but as the man who promised to protect her.

The man who loved her.

As much as he wanted to wish away those feelings now, he couldn't. Every inhale, he missed her. Every exhale, he grieved her. He was walking around his life like a ghost, already gone. He hated every moment of it.

He'd spent thirty years on this planet relatively happy, and generally led a pretty full life. Until he'd met Aria and realized exactly how empty and miserable all of it had been without her. In some ways, he barely knew her, but in others? It felt like half of him had been ripped away and he didn't know how to go on breathing without her.

Fuck. I sound like such a pussy.

Ben shook his head, trying to push the misery

away. This was not who he was. Ben Lawson was an independent, successful, experienced man who took command over his life, his career, and his relationships. At least, that was who he had been.

Picking up his phone one more time, he dialed Aria's number.

* * *

Aria glanced down at the screen on her new phone—a necessity after the insane volume of calls she'd received since yesterday. It was five minutes past the time the producer and director had said they'd come get her. The audition had gone really well, and despite all the misery of the last day, a tiny spark of hope was returning to her.

She had no doubt she could pull off this role. In some ways, she felt born to play it. A strong woman who risks everything for her art and her beliefs. It was everything Aria was raised to be, wanted to be, and strived to be.

"Miss Rose?" A young woman wearing a headset walked out into the hallway where Aria was sitting on one of the folding chairs that lined the wall. "Come on in."

"Thank you." Aria rose to her feet, smoothing out her dress and following the young woman as calmly as she could. Her stomach was flip-flopping, and her head was screaming, but she was worked damn hard to make sure none of that showed.

"Hello again, Miss Rose." The director

greeted her from a long desk on one side of the room where several people sat. "We won't keep you long. We just had a few questions."

She stood in front of them, her hands clasped together. "I'm happy to answer anything."

The director glanced at the man next to him, the producer, and a nervous energy passed between them that Aria immediately didn't like. "Well, honestly, you did an amazing job at your audition. You're clearly the best fit for the role we've seen so far."

Relief flooded her body. "Thank you so much."

"But—" He paused, and waited for the nod from the producer. "We're concerned about the current publicity. It's not the image we want for this movie."

Aria swallowed hard, but nodded. "I completely understand, sir. It's not the image I want for myself. Those photos...it wasn't with my permission. Police are already looking into it, and the studio I was last with is already removing them from sites. We're working hard to put it behind us as quickly and quietly as possible."

"Yes, that's a good start." The producer spoke up this time, tapping a pen against the surface of the desk. "But we definitely frown on on-set relationships because of this type of thing. We need a certain class of woman to play this particular role. I'm not entirely sure we're ready to cast you until we see how this plays out."

Aria tilted her head to the side. "Excuse me?"

"Like I said, you're absolutely perfect for the role," the director explained again. "But we're going to need some time to watch what direction this goes. You know how it is with the court of public opinion and all that."

"Are you...are you telling me I didn't get the part?" Aria tried to control her tone, but anger was starting to swell inside her. "Because of my personal life being exploited and illegally published online? Because being the victim of a complete invasion of privacy and sexual exploitation doesn't make me 'classy' anymore?"

"No," the producer quickly responded, alarm in his eyes. Probably because what he was saying was downright horrifying. "We're definitely not saying that. We all feel for you, Miss Rose. Truly."

Aria stood still for a moment and carefully looked around the room of men. They all stared back at her, looking uncomfortable and fidgety. An intern, a producer, a director, and some other administrative staff filled the small space and every single one of them was a man, the majority older than her own father.

Everyone but the young woman with the headset who'd led her into the room originally.

Aria's eyes came to a stop on her, but the woman looked away with just as much discomfort as her male counterparts. Aria wanted her to speak up. Help her. Defend her. *We are women, hear us roar.* "And you, ma'am? Are you okay with this?"

The woman swallowed, a lump pushing down her throat as she lifted her chin to stare Aria down. "Well, I'm not really the deciding vote—"

Aria shook her head, interrupting, "But, as a fellow woman, are you okay with this?"

A coldness entered the woman's gaze, and

she pushed her shoulders back. The original waver in her voice from moments before gone as she finally spoke her mind. "Well, Miss Rose, this studio *does* want to portray a certain image for this film, and for this character. I know *I* would never exchange sex for a promotion."

Fury suddenly built inside Aria, rolling waves of rage surging through her body. It was both exhausting and energizing all at once, and suddenly everything became very clear.

"You know what?" Aria shook her head. "I'm rescinding my interest in this project. Have a good day, folks."

"Wait!" The director jumped to his feet. "Miss Rose, please. Don't be hasty. You were fantastic! Very talented. Really, you'd be perfect for this part."

"I know." She stared pointedly back at him. "And for that reason — and that reason alone, — you should have given me the role."

He didn't have a response for that, and she didn't wait around for him to think of one. Her head held high, Aria walked out of the room with a new sense of confidence she'd never experienced before.

She deserved better — from this industry, from the press, from her fellow women, from it all. And she was going to fucking take it for herself. No more soft and sweet Aria Rose.

It was time to find her thorns.

CHAPTER TWENTY-SEVEN

"Thanks for coming by." Ben closed his front door behind the last visitor at the open house.

"I'm sorry, Mr. Lawson." The realtor he'd hired was piling her brochures together and putting them in her bag. "It's a great house—amazing location—but the architecture is...unique and the price point is high. It's just going to take some time."

"I understand. Thank you for all the work you're doing," Ben replied, showing her out. The open house had been busy, but ultimately, no one had been interested enough to even take a brochure, let alone fill out an application.

Ben walked across the cold marble foyer and headed for his office. The sooner he could be out of this house, the better. It didn't fit who he was. It never had. When he'd been married to Marion, they were a power couple—at least, that's what she always liked to call them—and this house had fit that image they'd created for themselves. It was in every way...powerful.

Ben had liked that picture once upon a time, but now he realized that's all he'd liked. None of it had been real. He'd been living a lie. Finding himself, finding the truth...it had all started when he'd decided to take the first step and divorce Marion. The job at Shepherd Films had been the next step toward finding who he wanted to be.

But Aria? She'd been an unexpected step, and, yet, she was the person who'd taught him the most. She was soft and nurturing, but she could command a room, not only with her talent, but with who she was. There was a selflessness to her and a kindness about her that he admired, and he could see so many others did as well.

She may not want anything to do with him anymore, but he wanted everything to do with her. He wanted to take everything she'd taught him, everything she'd inspired in him, and reflect that in his life going forward. He was already scouting new homes on the ocean—warmth and light being his top two requirements.

Grief squeezed his heart as he sat down at his desk. He'd never known it was possible to miss someone as much as he missed her.

He logged onto his computer and pulled up his email. Opening his draft folder, he pulled up the same email he'd been working on for weeks. The one he desperately wanted to send her, but just...couldn't.

She didn't want to hear from him. He wanted to respect that, but...damn it, it felt wrong. What they'd had, what they'd felt, or at least, what he'd felt...how could she just walk away from that?

How could she not be missing him as badly as he was missing her?

Clicking away from the email, he saved it back to his drafts. She needed more time, and he needed...he just needed her. That just wasn't an option right now.

Switching over to his inbox, Ben noticed that Arthur had sent him a website link. He clicked on it and Aria's picture appeared on the screen.

Dear Hollywood, Do Better.
Our Daughters Are Watching.

Boys will be boys, they said, and then they turned to me and called me a slut for the exact same thing. They critiqued every part of my body, broke me down piece by piece like cattle at an auction. The graphic comments from men, the disparaging remarks from women. No one had a kind word. No one had empathy. I read every comment, ingested that hate, and let it poison me. I let it make me question who I was, and who my mother and father had raised me to be.

Until I didn't.

Until I looked in the mirror and realized that the actions of one man changed nothing. What he did, how the press ran with it, how the public reacted...it hurt. It hurts so much, but it changed nothing.

I know who I am. I love who I am.

That's the lesson we should be teaching the next generation of women. That's the moral we could tell at the end of this story—rather than slut shaming, body shaming, or any other type of shame. Hollywood could use movies and films to lift women up, to empower an entire gender, and foster sisterhood and empathy for one another. They could lift the spirits of everyone who was ever told they're held to a different standard than their counterparts because of the body parts they were born with.

Judge me for my spirit. Judge me for my attitude. Judge me for my talent on the silver screen, but don't judge me for being a victim. I'm not, and you won't make me.

Aria Rose

Ben devoured every word in Aria's open letter in People Magazine. His heart both roared to life and shattered to pieces as he read. Pride swelled in his chest at her strength, inhaling deeply. In the same moment, every part of him ached to hold her. To take away the pain behind every word she'd written.

She'd laid herself bare in front of the world in an entirely different way, and refused to apologize for it. He loved her so much more in this moment than he'd ever thought possible.

The comments section was in the thousands already—so much of it positive and commending her—but it was an editor's note at the bottom that caught Ben's attention.

The author would also like to thank Shepherd Film Studios for their swift action in not only denouncing the actions of Russell Rains, director, and removing him from their current project, but assisting in the police investigation regarding his release of nonconsensual, intimate photographs of the author.

Waves of relief and sadness tumbled through him as he sat back in his chair. So, she'd seen what he'd done, how he'd tried to fix his mistakes, and yet, she still hadn't reached out to him. It had changed nothing for her.

Not that he'd done it for that reason, because he certainly had not. He'd done it because it was right, and because he wasn't going to run a company that would be associated with such vile behavior. Rains had received a small settlement for the work he'd done, and been removed from the project immediately. Ben had been the first person down at the police station giving a statement to aid in their investigation.

Thankfully, he wasn't being held legally responsible, though he'd told the police exactly what he'd done and what a drastic error he'd made. Law enforcement only had their eyes on Russell, because the victim had refused to press charges against anyone but him.

She'd saved him, both legally, and in the press, with her statement.

He'd promised to be there for her—no matter what. He was supposed to have protected her, and not only did he fail spectacularly at that, but she'd had to come to *his* rescue.

Ben opened up his draft folder one more time and pulled up the email he'd been wanting to send for two weeks. Finally, he clicked send.

Aria,

I should have told you weeks ago. I was wrong — so wrong. Don't forgive me. I just needed you to know. I'm sorry.

Ben

He wanted to say more. He wanted to tell her he should have chased after her and begged her forgiveness. He wanted to tell her he couldn't stop thinking about her, and that he'd read her article and seen her in the press and was so damn proud of her. He wanted to praise her for championing women, standing tall in the face of such adversity.

But telling her any of that would have been for him. To ease his guilt, his heartbreak. She deserved better than having to appease his pain.

Suddenly, an idea hit him. Ben grabbed his phone and scrolled through his contact list until he found the number he needed.

After two rings, the other side picked up. "Hello?"

"Hi, Travis. It's Ben Lawson. I've got a new project I'm about to start, and I'd like your help with it."

"A new movie?"

Ben shook his head, even though Travis couldn't see him. "Not exactly. Can you come by the offices first thing Monday morning? We need to move quickly on this."

"Sure. I'll see you then."

Ben was about to hang up, but then quickly

added, "Hey, Travis. One last thing—if you're still in contact with Aria, please don't mention anything about this to her."

"Uh...okay. Strange, but I can do that."

"Thanks, man. See you Monday." Ben hung up the phone feeling a surge of excitement, closing his computer. He stood and grabbed his keys, then headed for his car.

Ben dropped into the driver's seat and then scrolled through his contacts again, dialing another number this time. "Arthur, meet me at Shepherd Films."

"What? It's Saturday. I've got plans with a nine iron."

"See you in thirty minutes," Ben replied, ignoring him. "We've got a lot to do, and a really short amount of time to get it all done."

Arthur sighed, clearly exasperated. "Bloody hell. See you in thirty."

Ben gunned the car and raced out of his driveway. It would be a miracle if he could pull off his idea, but if he could, it would not only be fantastic for the studio, but for Aria and the film as well.

An invigorated sense of purpose came over him, inspired by Aria's article. For the first time since taking this job, Ben felt a true excitement for his position. He could do more than just make movies.

He had the power to change things, and that was exactly what he planned to do.

CHAPTER TWENTY-EIGHT

"Oh, Aria." Betty Reynolds sighed, her hands over her heart. "You look stunning. Absolutely perfect."

Aria twirled slowly on the platform, standing in front of three mirrors in the dressing room of a high-end gown shop in the heart of Beverly Hills. "Do you really like it?"

"Girl, *'like it'* doesn't do this dress justice." Steele came up behind her and fluffed out the back her dress, letting the short train fan out perfectly around her.

Dark, emerald green with sparkling crystals sewn into the bodice, the long gown wrapped around her neck and completely covered the front of her torso, while leaving her entire back bare. It stopped right above her butt, and thanks to double-sided tape, there were no worries of it dipping lower.

"I mean, the color alone is perfect," Steele continued. "With your pale skin and blond hair, it's such an amazing contrast. My brain is already kicking into overdrive right now thinking about what I'm going to do for your makeup."

"Mom, this isn't too much? It's just a premiere..."

"Sweetheart, this is your *first* premiere for your *first* movie as the starring lead. There's no dress that could ever be too much for that, plus this dress is perfect red carpet material."

"Best Dressed List without a doubt," Steele agreed. "And think of Ben's face when he sees you. Ooh, talk about revenge!"

"Steele!" Aria admonished, even though her romance with Ben was certainly no secret with these two. "I do *not* want revenge on Ben. I'm over him."

"What's that have anything to do with it?" Steele teased. "I want all my exes to miss me every moment of every day for the rest of their miserable lives. Serves them right for losing the best they ever had."

"Jesus H. Christ. Aria, don't take advice from this woman." Her mother pointed at Steele and gave her an annoyed look.

Steele just stuck her tongue out at her. "Unless it's about makeup."

Aria laughed. "You two love each other. Stop pretending to fight."

"We're not fighting," Steele replied.

"We're not," Betty agreed. "Except about getting revenge on exes. If you've moved on, great. Don't pay him any mind on the red carpet."

"I might have to take a picture or two with him..." Knots formed in Aria's stomach as she thought about it. She hadn't seen Ben in several months, and she was dreading the moment. Her anger had barely dissipated, despite the fact that it felt like so long ago now.

The last two months had been a whirlwind of press and attention that, thanks to her mother, she'd been able to spin in a pretty positive direction. She'd taken what had happened to her and used it as a platform to speak about gender equality and women's rights.

When the media discovered Russell had been let off the hook with only a $2,500 fine from the state of California for 'revenge porn,' there had been an absolute uproar from women's organizations across the country. He'd been blacklisted from every studio in Hollywood and ended up moving to New York City where, last she'd heard, he was trying unsuccessfully to get a job directing an indie film.

The support for her had been overwhelming and what had initially been a slut-shaming witch hunt had turned into a female empowerment campaign.

Aria couldn't be prouder to be able to spearhead the movement. She and her sisters, with the guidance of their mother, had even started their own non-profit to help actresses find equal representation in Hollywood, and ensure their rights were being protected on the job, as well as raising awareness and conducting self-affirmation outreach for young women looking to break into the business.

It was the start of a new chapter in her life, and she was unbelievably excited for all of it. She'd even secured several auditions in the coming weeks for movies with themes that supported her new mission. Her entire future was starting to take shape, and she felt enriched by the experience.

And yet, her heart ached when she went to bed at night in the apartment she'd spent so many nights with Ben. She hated that she had re-read his email to her no less than five thousand times. She'd picked up the phone to call him again and again, but stopped. The facts still remained the same—as sorry as he was, he'd still betrayed her. How did she get past that?

If she knew the answer to that, then maybe she'd call. Until then, she felt mired in her anger toward him. She couldn't forgive him...even if some part of her really wanted to.

Steele held still a tall pair of emerald stilettos and helped her step into them. Aria wiggled her toes into each, and waited as her friend strapped them.

"Are you going to be okay with seeing him tomorrow?" Her mother rubbed her upper arms comfortingly. "You looked so sad when we mentioned him."

Aria looked at her mother in the mirror's reflection. "I am sad, I think. I really, really liked him, and he completely destroyed that...but I'll be okay."

Betty sighed and shook her head. "Love is a tricky thing."

"We weren't in love," Aria lied, not wanting to admit it out loud—even to her mother. Hell, the idea was crazy, anyway. Their relationship had been so intense that she might just have confused it with love. "We weren't together long enough for that."

Her mother shrugged. "I knew I loved your father on our second date."

"I knew Xavier was 'the one' two weeks in," Steele chimed in, standing after she'd finished with Aria's shoes. "I was probably head-over-heels in love with him even sooner than that."

"Really?" Aria twirled in the mirror again, checking her dress from every angle with the height of her shoes.

"When you know, you know. Look at your father and me now—almost thirty years together." Her mother held up her cell phone and took a picture of her in the dress. "Gorgeous. I'm going to show him when we get back. The old man can't figure out texting."

Aria and Steele both laughed at that, but then Steele got back to business. "So, are we a 'go' on the dress? Honestly, we don't have time to find another one and get it fitted."

"We don't need to. I love it." Aria stepped off the platform and both Steele and her mother helped her get it off over her head and onto the rack. "You'll be over around noon to do hair and makeup?"

"Yeah, just text me the room number at the hotel."

Aria nodded, having already booked a hotel close by so they wouldn't travel far in her dress and would have the space to get ready. "I will."

"And go to bed early tonight and sleep in tomorrow. No circles under those eyes," Steele instructed. "You, too, Mama Reynolds. If I'm doing you and all the sisters, I need happy canvases."

Betty laughed. "So demanding."

"The best always is," Steele called over her shoulder as she rolled the rack with the dress out of the fitting room, since she'd be steaming it and bringing it to the hotel tomorrow.

Aria got dressed in the jeans and T-shirt she'd arrived in. "Ready, Mom?"

She was excited to get to the hotel and have a girls' night-in with her sisters, but even more excited for tomorrow. Strangely enough, after talking to her mother and Steele, the thing that excited her most had nothing to do with her first red carpet as lead actress or the movie screening.

A thrill rushed through her at the very thought of seeing Ben...his chiseled jaw, dark hair, and rugged masculinity. The way he'd felt with his arms wrapped around her, his body pressing down on top of her, pushing inside her...the memories warmed every part of her body.

The anger she felt toward him only seemed to spear her desire further, like she couldn't tell where her rage ended and passion began. She'd spent months trying to keep those thoughts and feelings at bay, but now...

Aria swallowed hard, shoving away the ache in her chest as she suddenly worried she wasn't as over Ben as she'd been telling herself.

CHAPTER TWENTY-NINE

"ARIA, LOOK OVER HERE!" Ben watched as photographers shouted for Aria to turn this way and that, lights flashing all over the red carpet. Smiling seductively, she peered back over her right shoulder at them, one hand on her hip.

She hadn't seen him yet, and he was happy to keep it that way for a moment. Watching her like this, strong and confident, adorned in diamonds and a gorgeous emerald gown...it was everything he'd ever wanted for her. This was her moment, and she looked like she'd been destined for it her entire life.

"ARIA, TAKE ONE WITH HIM!" a photographer shouted, pointing at Ben.

Aria's eyes widened, a glimmer of fear crossing her face when she turned to see where the photographer was pointing. Her shoulders relaxed when she saw him, however, and she gave him a small, tentative smile.

Ben approached her slowly, trying to calm the nerves in his stomach. "Hello, Aria."

She tilted her head to the side slightly. "Hello, Ben."

"Can I give you a hug?" He stretched his arms out, inviting her in.

"Sure." She slid her arms around his waist and he hugged her to his chest, despite the frenzy of cameras going off behind them.

It was only a few seconds before they let go, but it felt a million times longer and absolutely too short at the same time. Everything about her felt exactly like he remembered—warm and soft, delicate and tough.

She has to feel this, too.

Or maybe he just wished she was. Ben's mind raced as he considered everything that was about to happen. The movie premiere. His secret project. Travis's daring help.

"Let's take a picture together." She pulled away quickly, but left one arm wrapped around his waist as they both turned to the photographers and smiled. "For the fans."

"Sure. Just for the fans."

He wasn't buying her excuse.

A few minutes later, the cast and crew, along with the members of the press, were seated in the theatre as the opening credits for *Scarlet's Letters* began to roll.

Ben sat a row behind Aria, a few seats away, and overly aware of her presence. Sitting behind Aria for two and a half hours was literal hell. Being this close and still not being able to touch her, hold her, kiss her...damn, it was near impossible.

He barely paid attention to the movie. He didn't really need to since he'd seen it before the screening several times as the studio prepped it for release. Instead, his eyes were on her. The way she tilted her head back when she laughed, or brushed her fingers against her cheek to wipe away a tear. She was everything he remembered and more, and he was even more certain now than ever before that she was the only woman he'd ever love until the day he died.

She was it for him.

Ben waited for the final credits to roll, breathless for her to discover what he'd put together for the end. Not because he wanted her to come running back to him—though he'd definitely never turn her away—but because they were going to change lives, and she'd been the inspiration for it. Ben couldn't help but wish his father was here tonight, because he'd always told him *this* was the point of art.

The paycheck, the fame, the attention...it was nothing compared to the chance to impact people in a real way. To impact the world.

* * *

This is so surreal. Aria was fairly certain she'd never get used to moments like this. Standing on the red carpet earlier had been crazy enough, but here she was watching the credit roll after the screening of her very first big-budget film.

"That's you!" Tegan, Aria's sister, grabbed her arm and pointed to the big screen. Aria's name was displayed directly beneath Travis, who was seated on her other side, the followed by the rest of the cast.

A few months ago, she hadn't been sure she still had a career, and a few years ago, no one had known her name. Now her name was on a giant silver screen in front of the most influential names in Hollywood.

"So exciting!" Aria whispered back to her sister, then squeezed Travis's hand. "Travis, that was amazing! You were fantastic!"

"You were even better!" Travis whispered to her. "I'm so fucking nervous!"

"Why? It's over!"

He held her hand between both of hers, leaning closer to her. "It's just beginning. This is it, Aria."

"This is what?"

"The moment everything changes," he replied, then turned and gave a thumbs-up sign to Ben who was sitting a row behind them. "The moment the entire world learns who we are. Who I am."

Aria looked between them, then back at the screen, completely confused. Ben nodded back at Travis, smiling that rugged, sexy smile that made her stomach flip flop with excitement. Her skin felt like it'd been on fire since the moment he'd touched her, and concentrating on anything else was becoming increasingly difficult.

Hugging him on the red carpet had been almost too much for her. He'd felt comfortable...safe. The feeling caught her off guard, since she'd spent the last two months thinking the exact opposite.

"What's going on, Travis?" she asked, turning away from Ben. Clenching her jaw, Aria tried to find her anger toward Ben. Tried to find the pain she'd once felt at his betrayal. How he'd been just like every other man in her life. But...something didn't feel very real about that anymore.

"Watch the screen," he whispered back, pointing to where the credits were just ending, the lights in the theater still dim.

The audience suddenly gasped, and Aria's mouth fell open.

Travis appeared on the screen, completely nude except for skin-colored undergarments and a giant red "A" painted on his chest. He held a sign by his side, but didn't have it turned to face the camera just yet.

One-by-one, every single person from the *Scarlet's Letters* cast walked into the frame. Everyone except her because she had no idea what on earth was going on.

Each person wore only skin-colored underwear, or pasties, and a painted "A" on their chests, a sign by their side. A montage began to play, each person individually holding up different signs to the camera.

"No one will love you until you lose weight."

"Get a real job—passion doesn't pay the bills."

"You'll never be more than an ex-con."

"His life was worth more than mine."

"If you didn't want it, you shouldn't have dressed like a whore."

"Show me how badly you really want this part. On your knees."

Everyone who held their signs looked deeply emotional, and just from watching it, Aria felt the realness of their pain. She felt the vulnerability these people so bravely displayed to shine a light for others, to lead the way for aching hearts and forgotten souls. These were real...words that had actually been spoken to every person on that screen.

Her heart shattered for them, and at the same time, for herself. A cathartic release of everything people had called her over the last few months swelling inside her.

Travis returned on the screen next, and he held up his sign.

"Faggot."

One word. So simple. So full of meaning.

Aria burst into tears and threw her arms around Travis's neck, hugging him tightly. He was crying as well, but smiling proudly, his gaze still on the screen.

The audience murmured, and gentle sobbing could be heard among the crowd.

She couldn't even begin to put words to the amount of pride she was feeling for her friend right now. He'd just come out to the entire world in one of the bravest ways possible, and she could only imagine how much this moment meant to him.

As the music reached a crescendo, the cast returned in the frame together again and lifted their signs in front of them at the same time. A website and non-profit organization was written across each sign that said it was collaborating with Shepherd Films to promote human rights, treating everyone with respect and dignity, and ending shaming in Hollywood.

Aria couldn't believe it. *Did Ben put this together?*

She got her answer seconds later when Ben joined the cast. Completely naked except for skin-toned underwear, he stepped onto the screen with a sign that read *"we can do better."* Then he gave a ten-second summary of the organization and how viewers could help and donate.

It was a line from her article, and she knew then and there that she'd inspired this. He'd done this for her, or because of her. Either way, *this* was the Ben she knew.

This was the Ben she'd fallen in love with.

She just wasn't sure how to reconcile this wonderful man with the man who'd sold her photos to the tabloids for ticket sales.

Tears streamed down her face as Travis whispered to her, explaining how it had all come about and that Ben was the one behind it. The video would play at the end of every showing of the movie across the country, as well as a regular commercial on television for the next few months to aid the non-profit and its cause, all thanks to him.

She glanced back to look at Ben, not even bothering to wipe the tears from her cheeks. He stared at her, unmoving, his eyes dark and tumultuous. They stayed like that for a moment, just staring at each other — communicating everything and nothing in a gaze.

Finally, she mouthed, *thank you.*

Ben gave her a small nod, but nothing more. He didn't seem to want the praise, and he didn't seem to be using this as some tool to win her back. He just seemed proud, as he should be.

As she was for him, for herself, for Travis.

It was truly a big night for all of them, and she was only just now realizing all that really meant.

Everyone in the theatre began clapping as the screen finally went black and the lights turned on. Before she knew it, people were getting to their feet. The room roared with applause—a standing ovation not just for the clip at the end, but for the entire movie. For what all of it combined had stirred inside each and every person in that audience.

Aria felt it in the air and on the smiles on all the faces around her. *This is surreal.*

And it's just the beginning.

CHAPTER THIRTY

Aria entered the hotel ballroom after changing upstairs in her suite. She had loved her gown, but she couldn't dance in it. She'd opted for a shorter cocktail dress for the after party that was the same color, but had a skirt that swirled around her thighs as she moved.

"Aria!" Travis ran up to her and gave her a hug. "I just saw that the L.A. Times is already rating it one of their favorite movies of the year!"

"Wow!" The screening had only just ended an hour ago, so word was traveling fast. Aria was absolutely thrilled, not only because she'd truly felt like *Scarlet's Letters* was some of her best work, but because the movie was inspiring and she wanted everyone to see it. "This is going to be huge."

"I told you." Travis wrapped an arm around her waist and led her further into the party. "This is just the beginning."

She smiled at her best friend and laid her head against his shoulder. "I'm so glad I got to do this with you."

"Me, too, girl." He kissed her cheek. "But you know what this means, right?"

"What?"

Travis squeezed her to his side and made a super serious face. "We've got to break up."

"No!" Aria mocked, pretending to be shocked. "Travis Peters, do not tell me you're going to break my heart when I'm head-over-heels in love with you!"

He put a hand to his chest. "I know. I'm such a lady-killer. It pains me to say this, but we'll always have Paris."

Aria laughed. "We've never been to Paris!"

"Oh. Right. Then, we've got nothing, and you're just going to have to find some way to get over me." Travis grabbed her face and kissed her right on the lips. "Goodbye, darlin'," he said in a funny, old-Hollywood voice straight out of black-and-white movies. "Wish me luck out there."

"I'll never forget you, lover." She used her best Elizabeth Taylor impression. "Never!"

They both dissolved into giggles, hugging each other tightly.

"Seriously, Aria. I can't thank you enough," Travis whispered in her ear.

"You don't need to," she whispered back, and she completely meant it. They'd find a way to come clean to the press about their fake relationship, and she had no doubt it would all be fine. And if it wasn't? Well, she still didn't regret helping one of her best friends. "Love you."

Travis kissed her cheek. "Love you, and as much as I'd love to spend the whole party shaking it with you, there is a hottie in the corner who's been giving me 'the eye' all night."

Aria followed his gaze to another actor raising a glass of champagne in their direction. "Oh, he's cute. Go!"

"I'll talk to you tomorrow?"

"You'd better." She laughed as she watched him walking nonchalantly to his admirer, knowing he was actually probably nervous as hell.

"If your dance card is empty..." A voice behind Aria caused her to spin around, finding Ben standing there in his tux, offering her his hand. "I'd love this dance."

The corners of her lips twitched into a smile. She slid her hand in his, no longer trying to ignore the spark of electricity that happened every time they touched. Her other hand rested against his chest as he wrapped an arm around her and pulled her to him.

They swayed gently in the middle of the dance floor, a slow song playing as the party was still in its early stages.

Aria leaned her head against his shoulder. "That was an amazing thing you did, Ben."

He squeezed her a little tighter. "I didn't do much. You were the inspiration. Your article...it was amazing, Aria." Ben pulled away just far enough to look her in the eye. "You're amazing."

"Ben..." Heat infused her cheeks, and she dropped her gaze as her insides began to flutter with nervous energy. As angry as she still was over what he'd done with her photos, the same desire she'd felt with him from the start was just as strong. She was overwhelmed by how badly she wanted to kiss him and never let go, and how terrifying that idea seemed. "I...I..."

The words froze in her throat, her nerves increasing as she realized this could be entirely one-sided. Aside from one email, he hadn't tried to contact her at all. She'd told him not to, of course, but it still left her completely unsure of how he felt.

And how she felt? God, she had no clue.

"What is it?" he prodded her. The palm of his hand brushed against her cheek and she leaned into it.

Looking up at him from beneath her lashes, she let out a shuddering breath. "I miss you, Ben. I *really* miss you."

"You do?" Ben's brows lifted for a moment, surprised. "You miss me?"

She nodded her head slowly. "But..."

Swallowing, she paused for fear she'd burst into tears or be completely swallowed by the emotional moment. "But...I'm *so* angry, Ben. I'm so angry at you. You hurt me—badly. You completely betrayed me, and I'm just...I'm so angry."

Ben's eyes leveled with hers. "Good."

"What?" She blinked in confusion. That wasn't the response she'd been expecting, despite the fact that she felt a million times better having gotten all of that off her chest. In fact, it wasn't until right then that she'd realized just how angry she was and how badly she'd needed to say it to his face.

"I'm glad you're angry at me. You have every right to be. I deserve every bit of it, and you deserve to feel it. Do not let me off the hook for what I did, Aria. But..." He took the pause this time, shaking his head slightly, his face twisting in pain. "But don't let me go. Please. Make me earn back your trust. Make me do whatever you need for me to show you *that* isn't who I am. I'll do anything, but please, Aria...don't make me go."

She searched his eyes, aching at the suffering she saw behind them. "I...I don't want you to go."

Her admission surprised her as much as it did reassure her.

"Thank fucking goodness," Ben said, his face spreading into a wide smile. His hand slid to the back of her head and he crashed his lips to hers so fast she didn't even have a chance to breathe.

She let him dip her backwards as he kissed her with a dizzying passion, gripping her arms around his neck to hold on. His tongue pressed between her lips, and she parted for him, inviting him in to every part of her. It was everything she remembered, and everything she'd forgotten how badly she'd needed.

As absolutely sure as she was in that moment that she wanted to kiss him, wanted to feel him pressed against her, and wanted him to become a permanent fixture in her life, fear still swelled in her gut.

"Ben," she whispered against his lips. "We still need to talk. I have a room upstairs..."

He let out a low growl she felt rumble inside his chest. "What the hell are we still doing down here then?"

When they entered Aria's hotel room a few minutes later, their hands were all over each other.

She had so much she wanted to say, so much she wanted to tell him, but she couldn't find the words.

Instead, there was a fervor between them—heated and passion-filled need that made her ache for him even more than she already was. It was overwhelming, nearly drowning out the voice in the back of her head screaming—*danger!*

He slid her dress over her head, tossing it onto a nearby chair. The cold air made her skin pucker, a shiver running down her spine as she stepped out of her high heels.

She helped him unbutton his shirt and remove his tuxedo, all the while finding every possible second to press their lips to one another. It was like she couldn't stop kissing him. She couldn't stop needing him, and maybe she never had.

He lowered her onto the bed beneath him, and she let her eyes roam the length of his body above her. "God, Ben..." She licked her lips. "I've missed this."

"Me, too," he said with a groan, moving down her body and kissing every inch of her. His lips slid across her black bra and lace panties, and she writhed beneath him. Every bite, nip, kiss, lick pulled her further down, down, down, drowning in every inch of him until suddenly she gasped, needing to breathe.

"Wait!" Aria sat up quickly, pushing him off of her. "Ben. Stop."

He blinked, sitting back on his heels. His manhood was pressing against the front of his boxers very...obviously. Aria blushed and looked away.

"What's wrong?"

She shook her head, trying to figure out the answer to that very question. "This is what we do, Ben." She gestured between their bodies. "And then what?"

He chuckled, shrugging his shoulders. "Orgasms?"

"No. I mean, yes, but that's the problem. We haven't talked about anything. I just told you a few minutes ago how angry I am at you. I'm...I'm fucking livid, Ben. You can't charm your way out of that with..." Her eyes roamed his chiseled abs and the muscular lines that pointed down in a V to the top of his boxers. She motioned to his abs with a swirl of her wrist. "All that. I won't be distracted."

Ben laughed and sat back on the bed, getting comfortable. "Okay. No distracting you with my body. I got it." He reached down and picked up his undershirt and tossed it at her. "Here. Put that on."

"What? Why?"

"If you want me to focus, I can't be able to see your boobs. I'm only human, Aria." Ben smirked, and she rolled her eyes, laughing a bit.

She pulled on his shirt and sat back against the bed. "I'm not trying to be a buzz-kill here, and I am trying to see past what happened, but...it's hard. I thought what we had was so different, Ben. This was unlike anything I'd ever felt before."

Ben moved closer to her on the bed, pulling her against his side. "This *is* different. Aria, you and me are electric. We're everything you said you'd never believe in."

She raised one brow, curling into his side. "Soul mates?"

"Don't scoff. It's a real thing, and you're looking at it, baby."

Aria sighed, and kissed his chest when she wrapped her arm around him. They were both lying back on the bed, quietly staring at the ceiling, her leg and arm flung over his chest.

She still felt...unsettled. Fear still swarmed her stomach, and she couldn't break through whatever was keeping her from diving head first into a relationship with the man she lo — *did she love him?*

Ben broke the silence. "Aria, I can't tell you how sorry I am. When Russell showed me the pictures of you and Travis to leak to the press, I approved them without actually looking at the full roll of film. He told me to check them all. He made sure I signed papers saying I'd seen them all. The fact is...I lied. I saw two or three innocent photos of you and Travis, and, even knowing they were fake, I couldn't handle it. I couldn't look at all the pictures. If only I'd looked at the entire thing, none of this would have happened."

Aria pushed up against the mattress, propping herself up on her elbow. "You...you didn't see the photos?"

He shook his head. "Not until they were splashed across every tabloid in America. And I'm *so* sorry. It's completely my fault, and I will never forgive myself for it. Ever."

Aria shook her head, trying to make sense of it. "Ben, are you telling me you didn't purposefully leak the nudes of me? That wasn't a stunt for the movie?"

"WHAT?" Ben sat up, almost knocking her over. His eyes were wide, bewildered. "Aria, I would *never* do that to you. Not on purpose. Not for a movie. Not for a million movies. Not for any reason. Ever."

"God, Ben, I spent the last few months thinking you were exactly like every other power-hungry Hollywood exec who'd throw me under the bus to make a quick buck! Why didn't you tell me Russell was the one behind it?"

"I thought you knew," Ben said, rubbing his hands across his head and pushing his hair off his face. "Fucking hell. I'm going to kill Russell all over again."

"I knew Russell was the one leading the charge, but I thought you had gone along with his plan. I expected that kind of asshole stunt from him, but from you?" Aria felt her a lump swell in her throat, her voice breaking. "God, Ben. I was heartbroken."

Ben pulled her back down to the mattress, leaning over her and kissing down her jaw. He slid his tongue down the length of her throat, nipping her flesh along the way. "Aria, I'm so sorry. I'm sorry I let Russell do what he did. I'm sorry I didn't protect you. I'm sorry I didn't come find you immediately and explain it all. I'm sorry I ever let a minute go by that you didn't know exactly how much I love you."

She cupped his face in her hands, searching his eyes for any hint of doubt or insincerity but there was none. "You love me?"

Ben grinned his slightly crooked smile, his entire face lighting up in the process. "Head-over-fucking-heels, baby."

Aria kissed him, softly this time. Just her lips pressed to his, as if sealing their fate in the best possible way. "I love you, too."

Pushing her hips up against his, she kissed him again, but this time with heat. She'd waited long enough to feel his skin pressed against hers, and she wasn't going to waste one more moment of their lives together.

Sliding his undershirt over her head, she trembled as his fingertips caressed her skin as he moved down her body. Pushing her knees apart, he kissed her inner thighs until he reached her core. Aria nearly jolted off the bed at the contact, gasping and thrusting her hips against him harder.

Ben grinned up at her. "You're already soaked, Aria." He was rubbing his palm against her center, over the top of her lace panties. He gripped the edge, ripping them off her body entirely.

She heard the fabric tear, felt the cool breeze against her core, and then his mouth was on her and she wasn't sure she'd ever be able to breathe again. "Oh, my God!"

"Lay back, Aria. I've missed your taste too much to wait another second."

Aria swallowed hard as he dipped down between her legs and slid his tongue inside her. Moaning, she twisted her hands in the blanket beneath her and pumped her hips against his face greedily.

When he flicked his tongue across her length, her whole body jumped, and damn it, she wanted more. "Ben, I'm close..."

He picked up the pace, pushing harder against her as he licked and sucked until she tumbled over the edge, stars bursting in front of closed eyes, a wave of electricity pumping through her body so hard she wasn't sure if she was frozen or shaking uncontrollably.

When her climax finally began to wane, she went limp against the bedspread, blinking slowly as she stared at the ceiling. "Oh..."

Ben chuckled, climbing over her and positioning himself at her entrance. "I've *really* missed this, Aria."

Aria wrapped her arms around his neck, the exhaustion from seconds ago suddenly gone at the prospect of him inside her. "Now, Ben. I need you."

He growled, pushing his entire length inside of her.

She clenched tighter against him, pulling every inch of him into her and savoring the full sensation. Her legs wrapped around him, she pushed their bodies so far together, she was certain neither of them would know where they ended and the other began.

"I love you, Aria," Ben whispered to her again as he began slowly and methodically pumping in and out of her. "I love you so much."

"I love you," she replied, her lips pressed against his ear as she took him again and again.

Aria was suddenly hit with an emotional tidal wave, a desperation to hold on to the man she loved and never let go. Everything she'd pushed aside for months, weeks, days...swept away in a flood of truth as she realized that she wasn't just saying the words. She wasn't just in love with this man. She was meant to be with him.

Ben was the one, and for the first time ever, she could wholeheartedly admit that she believed in soul mates.

She believed in *them*.

EPILOGUE
TWO YEARS LATER

Ben glanced out the car window as they approached the red carpet entrance. "We're almost here. Two cars before us, then our turn."

"Ugh. I can't do this," Aria said from the seat next to him, leaning her head back against the headrest. "Ben, I can't go out there. Let's just go home."

"It'd take us another hour to drive all the way back to the beach, babe," Ben said with a laugh. They'd purchased their dream home overlooking the Pacific Ocean that was both expansive and cozy. For the first time, Ben understood what it meant to have a home, and that it was about so much more than four walls. "Aria, you can do this. You look beautiful."

"Don't lie to me, Ben. I know I look like a beached whale in rhinestones, okay?" Aria ran her hands over her swollen belly, which to him made her only that much more beautiful. How could he not find the mother of his future child breathtaking? "Do you know how many pins are holding me into this dress? I just got it fitted last week, and I'm already busting out of it."

Ben chuckled, pride filling him as the car moved closer to their destination. "Lawson men make big babies."

"Ben, I'm serious!" Aria huffed. "What if I can't get out of the damn car because I'm too big to fit through the door? What if my dress splits on stage? The press is going to rip me to pieces."

She was definitely beginning to spiral, and Ben didn't blame her one bit. This was her second time attending the Academy Awards and she was nominated for her first Oscar thanks to her most recent leading role in *Murals*. Last year, Travis had taken home the Oscar for Best Actor for *Scarlet's Letters*, and Aria had cheered him on the entire time.

She hadn't been nominated for that film last year, but had come back in a big way when Shepherd Films took over the production of *Murals* and cast Aria in the leading role solely based on her talent—something the press had finally stopped questioning after her stunning performance in *Scarlet's Letters*.

Though there was some stiff competition for the award tonight, Ben had zero doubt that Aria was taking home the award for Best Actress.

Similarly, he was on a career high with his release of two Academy Award worthy films in a row. The moment *Murals* had fallen apart after the original producers lost support when word got out about their sexist leadership, Shepherd Films had swooped in and purchased it at an amazingly low cost. Ben completely believed in the movie—he had since the first time Aria had mentioned it to him—and had been thrilled to see it become a box office hit.

Ben was also thrilled that he and his company were getting a reputation for philanthropic films and causes, opening the door for even more advocacy work in the future. He planned to keep making films that *meant* something, that inspired people—his own personal dream come true.

"Aria, look at me." Ben took her hands in his, pressing his forehead gently against hers. "You. Are. Beautiful."

"Ben..." She began to pull away, doubt crinkling the corners of her eyes.

"I'm serious, Aria." He caressed her cheek with his hand, cupping her face gently. "I couldn't be prouder to be starting a family with you, and you look downright gorgeous. You're glowing, baby."

She laughed, leaning forward to kiss him. Unfortunately, she couldn't lean forward very far because of her very-pregnant belly, and quickly gave up. "Kiss me," she said with an exasperated sigh. "Kiss me and tell me we're not absolutely insane. The new project, the new house, the baby...are we crazy?"

"Oh, we're definitely crazy." But he kissed her with everything he had. Life had certainly been full of unexpected surprises over the last few years—the baby being one of the biggest—but Ben was completely committed and excited about every part of it, and he knew Aria was, too.

They were both working on new films with noteworthy buzz in addition to their non-profit work, which was quickly gaining them the reputation of Hollywood's newest power couple.

But even if all of those wins were suddenly stripped away and all he had in this world was Aria standing next to him, holding his hand...it would still be the best damn life he could ever imagine for himself.

When Ben finally pulled away and broke their kiss, Aria's anxieties seemed miles away. Her smile wide, her body relaxed. She kissed him one more time, the smile never leaving her lips.

"Ready?" he asked.

She nodded. "As I'll ever be."

They pulled up to the red carpet, and Ben climbed out first. He turned quickly to help Aria out of the car and shield her from photographers until she was ready.

Smoothing her dress, she took his hand. "Well, I fit through the car door. So...there's that."

Ben laughed and squeezed her hand, lifting it to his lips and kissing the back of her palm. Her diamond ring jabbed his cheek slightly, but he didn't mind a bit because it was just another reminder that this was *his* woman.

This was his family, his future, his soul mate.

"I love you, Mrs. Lawson."

Aria looked up at him from under long lashes. "I love you, too, Mr. Lawson." She placed her other hand on her belly, gazing adoringly at it. "You're going to be so loved, Baby Lawson."

Ben grinned, his heart bursting in his chest at how beautiful and perfect his wife looked in that moment. "He has no idea."

"Or she," Aria reminded him.

Honestly, Ben would be happy with whatever life had in store for them. As long as he had his wife by his side.

Photographers caught wind of their arrival, and the flash of cameras began.

"ARIA LAWSON! BEN LAWSON! LOOK OVER HERE!"

"ARIA ROSE, WHEN ARE YOU DUE?"

"ARIA, TELL US WHAT IT WAS LIKE BEING THE BEST MAN AT TRAVIS PETER'S WEDDING LAST WEEK TO HIS HUSBAND?"

"ARIA ROSE, DO YOU THINK YOU'LL WIN BEST ACTRESS FOR *MURALS* TONIGHT?"

"ARIA, HOW DO YOU FEEL ABOUT BEING NAMED '*ACTIVIST OF THE YEAR*' BY ONE OF THE LARGEST WOMEN'S RIGHTS ORGANIZATION IN THE COUNTRY?"

The press shouted at them from behind a long metal fence. Aria smiled sweetly, posing both with Ben and by herself. She was already a pro, and he admired every second of watching her work the carpet. There was a grace to her that the press had finally begun to respect, and Ben loved how strong she was, and how she commanded respect from the very people who had once hung her out to dry.

No one was asking her about her sex life, or her nude photos, or even her outfit. They were asking about her career, her talent, her humanitarian efforts, her non-profit...they were focused on who Aria Rose was.

The women he admired more than any other.

The woman he was in love with, would raise a

family with, and grow old together.

The woman he'd married last year in a small, serene beach wedding that only one teenager chasing Pokémon had crashed.

Ben had never been prouder in his life to step back and let his better half take the spotlight.

She was a shining star, and he'd happily spend the rest of his life helping her burn brighter and brighter.

"Whatever our souls are made of, his and mine are the same." — *Emily Brontë*

ACKNOWLEDGMENTS

This book is uniquely special to me. It's actually the first book I've written in a while that I had 100% freedom on, and my soul flourished without limits. I actually wrote the entire first draft of this book in fourteen days.

The words just poured out of me.

This story isn't what it seems on the cover. Literally. And there's a reason for that. Judge a book by its cover...or maybe...don't. The perceptions and judgments we have of the people around us, people we meet online, people in magazines and on our television screens are powerful. They can be positive, and they can be horrifically destructive.

Here's a "fun" fact about this book...remember all those online comments you just read directed toward Aria? The slut shaming, the body shaming, etc? Each of those comments were not made up for this story. I found them on celebrity social media pages, online entertainment articles comment sections, and other online forums. Aside from slight editing for spelling and length, **those are real words said by real people.**

Not just men attacking women, but also, women attacking other women. I wove that into the story a few times because we can't blame this only on men when women so often lead the charge in tearing each other down. Hate is everywhere, and it doesn't need to be.

We all have the power to help. We have the power to change how we treat one another, and even how we treat strangers. We have the power to raise a new generation to do better than we've done, be kinder than we are, and more tolerant of everyone.

I hope after reading this story, you'll find yourself challenged to think a little differently about how, or if, we could be doing more to support our fellow sisters. If we could be doing more to bring an end to sexual exploitation and assault, gender gaps, and glass ceilings. If we could be doing more to spread kindness rather than rumors.

We are all the same once we are...nude.

Dear Humans, We Can Do Better...

* * *

To Kim Loraine, I couldn't have written this book without you. You were with my every step of the way, encouraging me to keep going and helping steer me to the finish line. Thank you, love.

To my agent, Nicole Resciniti, for supporting my solo efforts and being such a wonderful friend and confidante.

To Kay Springsteen Tate, for editing this novel and giving me the confidence to move forward. I always learn so much from you, and I'm so unbelievably lucky to have you on my team.

To each and every reader who has given me a chance over the years, and all the new readers who've just discovered me. You all are the reason I publish, and I'm so grateful for your unwavering support and kindness.

To all my 10,000+ best friend Skimmies, stop distracting me with such amazing stories and nonsense! I need to be writing! But also, thank you to Mallory Paul for the Pokémon Go suggestion—it made me laugh so hard that I had to include it in the book.

To Katherine Rochelle, you matter to me.

To Katie Crawford, you are so sweet and supportive. Thank you so much for always having my back and for helping me with this book. I value our friendship so much!

To my cronies, Amanda Oliver, Stephanie Krumm O'Reilly, and Trudy Larson...fuck you, guys. *middle finger emoji* (Ps: I love you more than I love cookie dough.)

To my best friend, Nicole Allen, for being so brave. I'm inspired by your courage and love.

To my husband, Justin, for finding your smile again. I love you, and I'm glad you get to see me nude.

ABOUT THE AUTHOR

Photo Credit: Valerie Bey

Sarah Robinson is the Top 10 Barnes & Noble and Amazon Bestselling Author of multiple series and standalone novels, including *The Photographer Trilogy*, *Kavanagh Legends* series, the *Forbidden Rockers* series, and *Not a Hero: A Marine Romance*. A native of Washington, D.C., Robinson has both her bachelor's and master's degrees in forensic and clinical psychology. She is married to a wonderful man who is just as much of an animal rescue enthusiast as she is, and together they own way too many animals to be considered sane.

OTHER BOOKS BY SARAH ROBINSON

The Photographer Trilogy
Tainted Bodies
Tainted Pictures
Untainted

Forbidden Rockers Series
Logan's Story: A Prequel Novella
Her Forbidden Rockstar
Rocker Christmas: A Holiday Novella
Her Dangerous Drummer

Kavanagh Legends Series
Breaking a Legend
Saving a Legend
Becoming a Legend
Chasing a Legend
Kavanagh Christmas

Standalone Novels
Not a Hero: A Bad Boy Marine Romance
Nudes: A Hollywood Romance

CONNECT ON SOCIAL MEDIA

booksbysarahrobinson.net
facebook.com/booksbysarahrobinson
twitter.com/booksby_sarah
instagram.com/booksbysarahrobinson
Snapchat: @booksbysarahrob

CPSIA information can be obtained
at www.ICGtesting.com
Printed in the USA
LVOW13s1526300617
539951LV00010B/606/P